I0656629

George John Whyte-Melville

Satanella

A story of Punchestown. Vol. 2

George John Whyte-Melville

Satanella
A story of Punchestown. Vol. 2

ISBN/EAN: 9783337301217

Printed in Europe, USA, Canada, Australia, Japan

Cover: Foto ©Andreas Hilbeck / pixelio.de

More available books at **www.hansebooks.com**

BY

G. J. WHYTE-MELVILLE

IN TWO VOLUMES
VOL. II.

LONDON
CHAPMAN AND HALL, 193, PICCADILLY
1872

CONTENTS OF VOL. II.

CHAPTER XXIX.

CHAPTER XXX.

CHAPTER XVI.

A GARDEN OF EDEN.

IN a comic opera, once much appreciated by
soldiers of the French nation, there occurs a
quaint refrain, to the effect that the gathering of
strawberries in a certain wood at Malieux is a
delightful pastime,

> " Quand on est deux,
> Quand on est deux—"

and the sentiment, thus expressed, seems appli-
cable to all solitudes, suburban or otherwise,
where winding paths and rustic seats admit of
two abreast.   But however favoured by nature,

the very smoothest of lawns, and leafiest of glades, surely lose more than half their beauty, if we must traverse them unaccompanied by somebody who makes all the sunshine, and perhaps all the shade, of our daily life.

To wait for such a companion is nevertheless an irritating ordeal, even amidst the fairest scenery, trying both to temper and nerves. It has been said that none realise the pace at which Time gallops, till they have a bill coming due. On the other hand, none know how slow he can crawl, who have not kept an uncertain tryst with over-punctuality "under the greenwood tree!"

General St. Josephs was not a man to be late for any preconcerted meeting, either with friend or foe. It is a long way from Mayfair to Kensington Gardens; it seemed none the shorter for an impatient spirit and a heart beating with anxiety and hope. Yet the old soldier arrived at the appointed spot twenty minutes too soon, there to suffer torments from a truly British malady called " the fidgets," while diligently consulting his watch and reconnoitering his ground.

How many turns he made, pacing to and fro, between the round pond and the grove, through which he longed to behold his goddess advancing in a halo of light and beauty, he would have been ashamed to calculate.

Some women never *can* be in time for anything, even for a lover; and after half an hour's waiting, that seemed a week, he drew a little note from his breast-pocket, kissed it reverently, and read it once more from end to end.

It said twelve o'clock, no doubt, and certainly was a very short epistle to be esteemed so sweet. This is what, through many perusals, he had literally learned by heart—

"My dear General,

"I want a long talk. Shall I find you in Kensington Gardens, where you say it's so pretty, at twelve o'clock?

"Ever yours,

"Blanche."

Now, in this composition, there appeared one or two peculiarities that especially delighted its recipient.

She had hitherto signed herself "B. Douglas," never so much as writing her Christian name at length; and here she jumped boldly to "Blanche," the prettiest word, to his mind, in the English language, when standing thus, like Falstaff's sack, "simple of itself." Also, he had not forgotten the practice adopted by ladies in general of crossing a page on which there is plenty of space, to enhance its value, as you cross a cheque on your banker, that it may be honoured in the right quarter. One line had Satanella scawled transversely over her note to this effect, "Don't be late; there is nothing I hate so much as waiting."

Altogether the General would not have parted with it for untold gold.

But *why* didn't she come? Looking round in every direction but the right, she burst upon. him, like a vision, before he was aware. If he started, and turned a little pale, she marked it, we may be sure, and not with displeasure.

It was but the middle of May, yet the sky smiled bright and clear, the grass was growing, butterflies were already on the wing, birds were singing, and the trees had dressed themselves in their fairest garments of tender, early green. She too was in some light muslin robe, appropriate to the weather, with a transparent

bonnet on her head, and a pink-tinted parasol
in her hand. He thought, and she *knew*, she
had never looked more beautiful in her life.

She began with a very unnecessary question.
"Did you get my note?" said she. "Of course
you did, or you wouldn't be here. I don't
suppose you come into Kensington Gardens
so early to meet anybody else!"

"Never did such a thing in my life!" exclaimed the General, quite frightened at the
idea—but added, after a moment's thought—
"It was very good of you to write, and better
still to come."

"Now what on earth do you suppose I wanted
to speak to you about?" she continued, in
rather a hard voice. "Let us turn down here.
I dare say you'd like all London to see us
together; but that wouldn't suit me at all."

This was both unprovoked and unjust, for

a more discreet person in such matters than the accused never existed. He felt hurt, and answered gravely, "I don't think I deserve *that.* You cannot say I have ever shown myself obtrusive or impatient with regard to *you.*"

"Don't look vexed," she replied; "and don't scold me, though I deserve it. I am in one of my worst tempers this morning; and who can I wreak it on but *you?*—the kindest, the bravest, the most generous of men!"

His features quivered; the tears were not far from his eyes. A little boy with a hoop stood still, and stared up in his face, marvelling to see so tall a gentleman so greatly moved.

He took her hand. "You can always depend on *me*," he said softly; and, dropping it, walked on by her side in silence.

"I know I can," she answered. "I've known it a long time, though you don't think so.

—What a hideous little boy! Now he's gone on with his hoop, I'll tell you what I mean.— One of the things that first made me like you, was this—you're a gentleman down to the heels of your boots!"

"There's not much in that," he replied, looking pleased, nevertheless. "So are most of the men amongst whom you live. A fellow ought to have something more than a good coat and decent manners, to be worthy of your regard;—and you *do* like me, Miss Douglas? Tell me so again. It is almost too much happiness for me to believe."

"That's not the question. If I hated anybody very much, do you think I would ask him to come and walk with me in Kensington Gardens at an hour when all respectable people are. broiling in the Park?" said she, with one of her winning laughs. "You're wrong, though, about the people in good coats. What I call a gentleman is—well—I can't think of many— King Arthur, for instance, in 'Guinevere.' "

"Not Launcelot!" he asked. "I thought you ladies liked Launcelot best."

"There are plenty of Launcelots," she answered dreamily, "and always will be. *Not Launcelot, nor another*, except it be *my* General!"

Could he do less than take her arm and press it fondly to his side?

They had loitered into the seclusion of a forest-glade, that might have been a hundred miles from London. The little boy had vanished with his hoop, the nursery-maids and their charges were pervading the broad gravel walks and more frequented lawns of this sylvan paradise; not a soul was to be seen threading the stems of the tall trees but themselves, and

an enthusiastic thrush straining its throat in
their ears, seemed to ensure them from all
observation less tolerant than its own.

"Now or never!" thought Satanella. "It
must be done; and it's no use thinking about
it!"

Turning round on her companion, she crossed
her slender hands over his arm, looked caress-
ingly in his face, and murmured—

"General, will you do me a favour?"

Pages could not have conveyed the gratification expressed by his monosyllable, "Try!"

She looked about, as if searching for some
means of escape, then said hurriedly—

"I am in a difficulty. I want money. Will
you help me?"

Watching his face, she saw it turn very
grave. The most devoted of lovers, even while
rejoicing because of the confidence reposed in

Go on, will you do me a favour?

him, cannot but feel that such a question must
be approached with caution—that to answer it
satisfactorily will require prudence, forethought,
and self-sacrifice. To do the General justice,
which Satanella at the moment did not, his
circumspection was far removed from hesitation; he had no more idea of refusing, than
the gallant horse who shortens his stride, and
draws himself together, for a larger fence than
common, that he may collect his energies, and
cover it without a mistake.

For one delightful moment Miss Douglas felt
a weight lifted from her heart, and was already
beginning to unsay her words as gracefully as
she might, when he stopped her, with a firm,
deliberate acquiescence.

"Of course I will! And you ought to know
by this time nothing can make me so happy
as to be of use to you in any way. Forgive

me, Miss Douglas—business is business—how much?"

Her face fell; she let go of his arm, and her lips were very dry, while she whispered, "Three thousand!"

· He was staggered, and showed it, though he tried hard not to look surprised. Few men can lay their hands on three thousand pounds of hard money, at a moment's notice, without some personal inconvenience. Now the General was no capitalist, though in easy circumstances, and drawing the half-pay of his rank; to him such an outlay meant a decreased income for the rest of his life.

She was quite right about his being a gentleman. In a few seconds he had recovered his composure; in half a minute he said quietly—

"You shall have it at once. I am only so glad to be able to oblige you, that I wish it

was more difficult. And now, Miss Douglas,
you always say I'm a sad fidget, I'll go about
it directly; I'll only ask you to come with me
to the end of the walk."

She was crying beneath her veil; he saw
the tears dropping on her hands, and would
have liked to kiss them away on any other
occasion but this.

"To the end of the world!" she answered,
with the sobs and smiles of a child. "There's
nobody like you—nobody!—not even King
Arthur! Ask what you will, I'll never refuse
you—never—as long as I live!"

But it need hardly be said that the General
would rather have cut off his right hand, than
have presumed on the position in which her
confidence had placed him. Though she appreciated his consideration, she hardly understood
why his manner became so unusually respectful

and courteous, why his farewell—under the
supervision of a cabman and a gate-keeper—
should be almost distant; why he lifted his
hat to her, at parting, as he would to the
Queen—but, while he replaced it on his bald
and grizzled head, Blanche Douglas was nearer
being in love than she suspected with this true,
unselfish admirer, who was old enough to be
her father.

In women, far more than in men, there can
exist an affection that springs from the head
alone. It is the result of respect, admiration,
and gratitude. It is to be won by devotion,
consistency, above all, self-control; and, like
a garden flower, so long as it is tended with
attention, prospers bravely till autumn cools
the temperature, and saddens all the sky. But
this is a very different plant from the weed,
wild rose, nightshade—call it what you will

—that is sown by the winds of heaven, to strike
root blindly and at haphazard in the heart;
sweeter for being trampled, stronger for being
broken, proof against the suns that scorch, the
winds that shatter, the worm that eats away
its core, and, refusing to die, even in the frown
of winter, under the icy breath of scorn and
unmerited neglect.

Which of these kindred sentiments the
General had succeeded in awakening, was a
problem he shrank from setting himself honestly
to solve. He tried to hope it might be the one;
he felt sadly convinced it was only the other.
Traversing the gardens with swift, unequal
strides, so as to leave them at the very farthest
point from where his companion made her exit,
for he was always loyal to *les convenances*,
he argued the question with his own heart,
till he dared not think about it any longer,

subsiding at last into composure, with the
chivalrous reflection, that, come what might,
if he could but minister to the happiness of
Blanche Douglas, he would grudge no sacrifice,
even :the loss of his money—shrink from no
disappointment, even the destruction of his
hopes.

Satanella meanwhile had selected a Hansom
cab, in which to make her homeward journey,
characteristically choosing the best-looking
horse on the stand. To be seen, however,
spanking along, at the rate of twelve miles
an hour, in such a vehicle, she reflected,
might be considered *fast* in a young unmarried
lady, and originate, also, surmises as to the
nature of her expedition; ' for it is quite a
mistake to suppose that people in London are
either blind or dumb, because they have so
much on hand of their own, that they cannot

devote all their attention to the business of their neighbours. With commendable modesty, therefore, she kept her parasol well before her face, so as to remain unrecognised by her friends, while she scanned everything about her with the keen, bright glances of a hawk. Bowling past Kingston House, then, and wondering whether it would not be possible, in time, to raise a domestic pedestal for General St. Josephs, on which she might worship him as a hero, if she could not love him as a Cupid, her Hansom cab passed within six inches of another, moving rapidly in the opposite direction ; and who should be seated therein, smoking a cigar, with a white hat and light-coloured gloves, but ruined, reckless, never-to-be-forgotten Daisy !

She turned sick, and white even to the lips. In one glance, as women will, she had taken in every detail of his face and person, had marked that the one seemed devoid of care, the other well-dressed, as usual. Like a stab came the conviction, that ruin to *him* meant only a certain amount of personal inconvenience, irrespective of any extraneous sorrow or vexation; and in this she misjudged him, not quite understanding a nature she had unwittingly chosen for the god of her idolatry.

Though they passed each other so quickly, she stretched her arms out and spoke his name, but Daisy's whole attention was engrossed by a pretty horse-breaker in difficulties on his other side. Satanella felt, as she rolled on, that he had not recognised her, and that if she acted up to her own standard of right, this miserable glimpse must be their last meeting, for she ought never to see him again.

"He'll be sure to call, poor fellow!" she

murmured, when she reached her own door. So it is fair to suppose she had been thinking of him for a mile and a quarter. " I should like to wish him good-bye, *really* for the last time. But no, no ! Honour, even among thieves. And I'm sure *he* deserves it, that kind, noble, generous old man. Oh ! I wish I was dead ! I wish I was dead ! " Then she paid the cabman (more than his fare), told her servant, in a strange, hoarse voice, that " she was at home to nobody this afternoon —nobody, not even Mrs. Lushington ! " and so ran fiercely up-stairs, and locked herself in her room.

CHAPTER XVII.

"SOLDIER BILL."

D AISY placidly smoking, pursued the even tenor of his way, thinking of the pretty horse-breaker more than anything else; while disapproving, in a calm, meditative mood, of her hat, her habit, her bridle, and the leather tassels that dangled at her horse's nose.

The particular business Mr. Walters had at present on hand in London, or rather Kensington, must be explained.

Perhaps it may be remembered how, in a financial statement made by this young officer during the progress of a farce, he affirmed that, should he himself "burst-up," as he called it, a certain "Soldier Bill" would become captain of that troop which it was his own ambition to command. With the view of consulting this rising warrior in his present monetary crisis, Daisy had travelled, night and day, from Ireland, nor could he have chosen a better adviser in the whole Army List, as regarded kindness of heart, combined with that tenacious courage Englishmen call "pluck."

"I'm not a clever chap, I know," Bill used to acknowledge, in moments of expansion after dinner. "But what I say is this: If you've got to do a thing, catch hold, and do it! Keep square, run straight, and ride the shortest way! You won't beat *that*, my boy, with all the dodges that ever put one of your nobblers in the hole!"

It is but justice to admit that, in every relation of life, sport or earnest, this simple
moralist acted strictly in accordance with his
creed. That he was a favourite in his regiment
need hardly be said. The younger son of a
great nobleman, he had joined at seventeen,
with a frank childish face and the spirits of
a boy fresh from school. Before he was a
week at drill, the very privates swore such a
young dare-devil had never ridden in their
ranks since the corps was raised. Utterly
reckless, as it seemed, of life and limb, that
fair-haired, half-grown lad, would tackle the
wildest horse, swim the swiftest stream, leap
the largest fence, and fight the strongest man,
with such rollicking, mirthful enjoyment, as
could only spring from an excess of youthful
energy and light-heartedness. But, somehow,
he was never beat, or *didn't know* it when he

was. Eventually, it always turned out that the horse was mastered, the stream crossed, the fence cleared, and the man obliged to give in. His warlike house had borne for centuries on their shield the well-known motto, "Go on!" To never a scion of the line could it have been more appropriate than to this light-footed, light-headed, light-hearted Light Dragoon!

In his own family, of course, he was the pet and treasure of all. His mother worshipped him, though he kept her in continual hot water with his vagaries. His sisters thought (perhaps reasonably enough) that there was nobody like him in the world. And his stately old father, while he frowned and shook his head at an endless catalogue of larks, steeple-chases, broken bones, &c., was more proud of Bill in his heart than of all his ancestors and all his other sons put together.

They were a distinguished race. Each had made his mark in his own line. It was "Soldier Bill's" ambition to attain military fame; every step in the ladder seemed to him, therefore, of priceless value, and promotion was as the very breath of his nostrils.

But a man who delights in personal risk is rarely of a selfish nature. In reply to Daisy's statement, made with that terseness of expression, that total absence of circumlocution, complimentary or otherwise, which distinguishes the conversation of a mess-table, Bill ordered his visitor a "brandy-and-soda" on the spot, and thus delivered himself.

"Troop be d—d, Daisy! It's no fun soldiering without your 'pals.' I'd rather be a Serrafile for the rest of my life, or a bâtman, or a trumpeter, by Jove! than command the regiment only because all the good fellows

in it had come to grief. Sit down. Never
mind the bitch, she's always smelling about
a strange pair of legs, but she won't lay hold,
if you keep perfectly still. Have a weed, and
let's see what can be done ! "

The room in which their meeting took place
was characteristic of its occupant. Devoid of
superfluous furniture, and with an uncarpeted
floor, it boasted many works of art, spirited
enough, and even elaborate, in their own particular line. The series of prints representing
a steeple-chase, in which yellow jacket cut
out all the work, and eventually won by a
neck, could not be surpassed for originality of
treatment and fidelity of execution. Statuettes
of celebrated acrobats stood on brackets along
the walls, alternating with cavalry spurs, riding-
whips, boxing-gloves, and basket-hilted sticks,
while the place of honour over the chimney-

piece was filled by a portrait of Mendoza in
fighting attitude, at that halcyon period of the
prize-ring,

"When Humphreys stood up to the Israelite's thumps,
    In kerseymere breeches, and ' touch-me-not ' pumps."

"It's very pleasant this," observed Daisy,
with his legs on a chair, to avoid the attentions
of Venus, an ill-favoured lady of the "bull"
kind, beautiful to connoisseurs as her Olympian
namesake, but for the uninitiated an imper-
sonation of hideous ferocity and anatomical
distortion combined.

"Jolly little crib, isn't it?" replied Bill; "and
though I'm not much in ' fashionable circles,'
suits me down to the ground. Wasn't it luck,
though, the smallpox and the regimental
steeple-chase putting so many of our captains
on the sick-list, that they detached a subaltern
here to command? We were so short of officers,

my boy, I thought the Chief would have made you 'hark back' from Ireland. Don't you wish he had? You'd better have been in bed on the 17th; though, by all accounts, you rode the four miles truly through, and squeezed the old mare as dry as an orange!"

"Gammon!" retorted Daisy. "She had five pounds in hand, only we got jostled at the run-in. I'll make a match to-morrow with Shaneen for any sum they like, same course, same weights, and—— But I'm talking non-sense! I couldn't pay if I lost. I can't pay up what I owe now. I'm done, old boy; that's all about it. When a fellow can't swim any farther, there's nothing for it but to go under!"

His friend pulled a long face, whistled softly, took Venus on his lap, and pondered with all his might.

"Look here, Daisy," was the result of his

cogitations; "when you've got to fight a cove
two stone above your weight, you don't
blunder in at him, hammer-and-tongs, to get
your jolly head knocked off in a couple of
rounds. No; if you have the condition (and
that's everything), you keep dodging, and waiting, and out-fighting, till your man's blown.
Then you tackle to, and finish him up before
he gets his wind again. Now this is just your
case. Ask for leave; the Chief will stand it
well enough, if he knows you're in a fix. *I'll*
do your duty, and you must get away some-
where, and keep dark, till we've all had time
to turn ourselves round."

"Where can I go to?" said Daisy. "What
a queer smell there is in this room, Bill. Something between dead rats and a Stilton cheese."

"Smell!" answered his host. "Pooh; non-
sense. That's the badger; he lives in the

bottom drawer of my wardrobe. We call him
'Benjamin.' Don't you *like* the smell of a
badger, Daisy ?"

Now, "Benjamin" was a special favourite
with his owner, in consideration of the creature's obstinate and tenacious courage. Bill
loved it from his heart, protesting it was the
only living thing from which he "took a
licking ; " because on one occasion, after a
very noisy supper, the man had tried, and failed,
to "draw" the beast from its lair with his
teeth ! Therefore, "Benjamin" was now a free
brother of the Guild, well cared for, unmolested,
living on terms of armed neutrality with the
redoubtable Venus herself.

Ignoring as deplorable prejudice Daisy's
protest that he did *not* like the smell of a
badger, his friend returned with unabated interest to the previous question.

"You mustn't stay in London, that's clear; though I've heard there's no covert like it to hang in for a fellow who's robbed a church! But it wouldn't suit *you.* You're not bad enough; besides, it's too near Hounslow. The Continent's no use. Travelling costs a hat-full of money, and it's very slow abroad now the fighting's over. A quiet place, not too far from home; that's the ticket!"

"There's Jersey," observed Daisy doubtfully. "I don't know where it is, but I daresay it's quiet enough."

"Jersey be hanged!" exclaimed his energetic friend. "Why not Guernsey, Alderney, or what do you say to Sark? No, we must hit on a happier thought than that. You crossed last night, you say. Does any one know you're in town?"

"Only the waiter at Limmer's. I had breakfast there, and left my portmanteau, you know."

"Limmer's! I wish you hadn't gone to Limmer's! Never mind; the waiter is easily squared. Now, look here, Daisy, you're not supposed to be in London. Is there no retired spot you could dodge back to in Ireland, where you can get your health, and live cheap? Who's to know you ever left it?"

His friend Denis occurred to Daisy at once.

"There's a farm up in Roscommon," said he, "where they'd take me in and welcome. The air's good, and living *must* be cheap, for you can't get anything to eat but potatoes! I shouldn't wonder if they hunted all the year round in those hills, and the farmer is a capital fellow, never without a two-year-old that can jump!"

"That sounds like it," responded the other, with certain inward longings of his own for this favoured spot. "Now, Daisy, will you ride to orders, and promise to be guided entirely by *me?*"

"All right," said Daisy; "fire away."

"Barney!" shouted his friend, in a voice that resounded over the barracks, startling even the sergeant of the guard. "Barney! look sharp. Tell them to put a saddle on Catamount, and turn him round ready to go out; then come here."

In two minutes a shock-headed bâtman, obviously Irish, entered the apartment, and stood at "attention," motionless, but for the twinkling of his light blue eyes.

"Go to Limmer's at once," said his master; "pay Mr. Walters's bill. Breakfast and B. and S., of course? Pack his things, and take them to Euston Station. Wait there till he comes, and see him off by the Irish mail. Do you understand?"

"I do, sur," answered Barney, and vanished like a ghost.

"You've great administrative powers, Bill," said his admiring friend. "Hang it! you're fit to command an army."

"I could manage the commissariat, I think," answered the other modestly; "but of course you're only chaffing. I'm not a wise chap, I know; never learnt anything at school, and had the devil's own job to pass for my cornetcy. But I'll tell you what I *can* do. When a course is marked out, and the stewards have told me which side of the flags I'm to go, I *do* know my right hand from my left, and that's more than every fellow can say who gets up for a flutter in the pig-skin! And now I'm off to head-quarters to see the Chief, and ask leave for you till muster, at any rate."

"You won't find him," observed Daisy. "It must be two o'clock now."

"Not find him!" repeated the other. "Don't you know the Chief better than that? He gets home-sick if he is a mile from the barrack-yard. It's my belief he was born in spurs, with the 'state' of the regiment in his hand! Besides, he's ordered a parade for fitting on the new nose-bags at three. He wouldn't miss it to go to the Derby."

"You *are* a good chap," said his friend. "It's a long ride, and a beastly hard road!"

Bill was by this time dressing with inconceivable rapidity, and an utter disregard of his comrade's presence.

"A long ride," he repeated, in high scorn, while he dashed into a remarkably well-made coat. "What do you call a long ride with a quad. like Catamount? Five-and-forty minutes is what he allows me from gate to gate ; and it takes Captain Armstrong all his time, I can tell you, to keep him back to *that!* The beggar ran away with me one night from Ashbourne to the Royal Barracks in Dublin; and though it was so dark you couldn't see your hand, he never made a wrong turn, nor let me get a pull at him, till he laid his nose against his own stable-door. Bless his chesnut heart! he's the worst mouth and the worst temper of any horse in Europe. Look at him now. There's a pair of iron legs, and a wicked eye! It's rather good fun to see him kick directly I'm up. But I've never had such a hack, and I wouldn't part with him to be made Commander-in-Chief."

Daisy could do no less than accompany his

host to the door, and see him mount this
redoubtable animal, the gift of a trainer at
the Curragh, who could do nothing with it,
and opined that even Soldier Bill's extraordinary nerve would be unequal to compete with
so restive a brute. He had miscalculated,
however, the influence utter fearlessness can
establish over the beasts of the field.

Catamount's first act of insubordination, indeed, was to run away with his new master for
four miles on end, across the Curragh, but over
excellent turf, smooth as a bowling-green: he
discovered, to his surprise, that Bill wished no
better fun. He then repeated the experiment
in a stiffly-fenced part of Kildare; and here
found himself not only indulged, but instigated
to continue, when he wanted to leave off. He
tried grinding his rider's leg against the wall:
Bill turned a sharp spur inwards, and made it

very uncomfortable. He lay down : Bill kept him on the ground an hour or two by sitting on his head. At last he confined himself to kicking unreasonably, at intervals, galloping sullenly on, nevertheless, in the required direction, and doing a vast amount of work in an incredibly short space of time. He was never off his feed, and his legs never filled, so to Bill he was invaluable, notwithstanding their disputes, and a certain soreness about a cup the horse ought to have won, had he not sulked at the finish : they loved each other dearly, and would have been exceedingly loth to part.

"My sergeant's wife will get you some dinner," said the rider, between certain preliminary kicks in getting under way. "She's an outside cook, and I've told her what you'd like. There's a bottle of brandy on the chimney-piece, and soda-water in the drawer

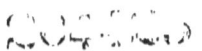

next the badger. I'll be back before it's time
for you to start. Cut along, Catamount! Hang
it! don't get me off the shop-board before half
the troop. Forrard, my lad! forrard away!"
and Bill galloped out of the barracks at headlong speed, much to the gratification of the
sentry manipulating his carbine at the gate.

This true friend proved as good as his word.
In less than three hours he was back again,
Catamount having hardly turned a hair in their
excursion. The Colonel had been kindness itself.
The leave was all right. There was nothing
more to be done, but to pack Daisy off in a
Hansom for Euston Square.

"Take a pony, old man," said Bill, urging his
friend to share his purse, while he wished him
"good-bye." "If I'd more you should have it.
Nonsense! I don't want it a bit. Keep your
pecker up and fight high! Write a line if any-

thing turns up. I'll go on working the job here, never fear. We won't let you out of the regiment. What is life, after all, to a fellow who isn't a Light Dragoon?"

CHAPTER XVIII.

DELILAH.

IN consoling his friend, *Xanthias Phoceus*, for the result of a little flirtation, in which that Roman gentleman seems to have indulged without regard to station, Horace quotes for us a triad of illustrious persons whose brazen-plated armour and bull's-hide targets were of no avail to fence them from the shafts of love. If neither petulant Achilles, nor Ajax, son of Telamon, nor the king of men himself, could escape, it is not to be supposed that a young cavalry officer in her Majesty's service, however simple in his habits and frank in his demeanour, should be without some weakness of the same nature, unacknowledged perhaps, yet none the less a weakness on that account.

"Soldier Bill," notwithstanding his kindly disposition and fresh comely face, seemed the last man in the world to be susceptible of female influence, yet "Soldier Bill" felt, to a certain extent, in the same plight as Agamemnon. Though in dress, manners, and appearance, anything but what is usually termed "a ladies' man," he was nevertheless a prime favourite with the sex, on such rare occasions as threw him in their way. Women in general seem most to appreciate qualities not possessed by themselves, and while they greatly admire all kinds of courage, find that which is mingled with good-humoured hap-hazard recklessness, perfectly irresistible. They worship their heroes

too, and believe in them, with ludicrous good
faith. Observe a woman in a pleasure-boat.
If there comes a puff of wind, she never takes
her eyes off the boatman, and trusts him implicitly. The more frightened she feels, the
more confidence she places in her guardian, and
so long as the fancied danger lasts, clings de-
votedly to the pilot, be he the roughest, hairiest,
tarriest son of Neptune that ever turned a quid.

Now the converse of this relation between the
sexes holds equally good. To live entirely
with men and horses; to *rough it* habitually
from day to day, enduring hardships voluntary
or otherwise, in the pursuit of field-sports; to
share his studies with a dog, and take his pastime with a prize-fighter, does not necessarily
unfit a man for the society of gentler, softer,
sweeter, craftier creatures. On the contrary, in
many natures, and those perhaps the strongest,

such habits produce a longing for female society, deeper and keener that it has to be continually repudiated and repressed. .

When he had started Daisy for the station, Bill renewed his toilet with peculiar care, and in spite of a few scars on his face, some the effects of falls, others, alas! of fights, a very good-looking young gentleman he saw reflected in his glass. Smoothing a pair of early moustaches, and sleeking a close-cropped head, he searched about in vain for a scent-bottle, and actually drew on a pair of kid gloves. Obviously, "Soldier Bill" was going to call on a lady. He could not help laughing, while he thought how the cornets would chaff him, if they knew. Nevertheless, with a farewell caress to the badger, fresh, radiant, and undaunted, he sallied forth.

It was quite in accordance with the doctrine

of opposites, propounded above, that Bill should
have experienced a sensation of refreshment
and repose in the society of a charming married
woman, very much his senior, who made light of
him no doubt, but amused, indulged, and in-
structed him while she laughed. Her boudoir
was indeed a pleasant change from his barrack-
room. He could not but admit that in *her*
society tea seemed a more grateful beverage
than brandy and soda; the tones of a piano-
forte sweeter than any stable-call; and the
perfume that pervaded every article about her
far more delightful, if less pungent, than that
which hung round his retiring friend "Benjamin," in the bottom drawer of the wardrobe.

In his wildest moments, however, Bill never
dreamed of making love to her; and it is not
difficult to understand that his goddess, being
no less experienced a person than Mrs. Lush-

ington, was well able to take care of her-self.

"I like the boy," she used to say to any one who would listen, even to her husband, if nobody else could be found. "He is so fresh and honest, and he looks so *clean!* It's like having a nice child about one, and then I can do him so much good. I form his manners, teach him the ways of society, prevent his being imposed upon, and generally make him fit for civilised life. If there were no good-natured people like me, Frank, these poor young things would fall a prey to the first designing girl who comes across them on the war-path, looking out to catch a husband *coûte que coûte.* I'm sure his mother ought to be infinitely obliged to me. She couldn't take more pains with him herself! When he began coming here, he didn't know how to waltz, or to take off his hat, or to answer a note even; in short, he couldn't say Bo to a goose! And now I've made him learn all these things, and he does them well, particularly the last. He's still absurdly shy, I grant you, but it's wearing off day by day. When I'm grown old, Frank, and wrinkled (though I'd sooner die first), he'll be grateful, and understand what care I've taken of him, and what a sad fate might have befallen him, but for *me!* Isn't there something in Doctor Watts, or somebody,

> ' Regardless of their doom,
> The little victims play ' ?

Frank! I don't believe you're listening!"

"Oh yes, I am," answers Frank, whose thoughts have wandered to Skindle's, Richmond, Newmarket—who knows where? "What you say is very true, my dear—very true—and nobody understands these things better than yourself. Good gracious! is that clock right!

I had no idea it was so late ! I must be off
at once, and—let me see—I'll get back to
dinner if I *can ;* but don't wait."

So *exit* Mr. Lushington on his own devices,
and enter a footman with tea, closely followed
by the butler ushering in " Soldier Bill."

"Talk of somebody," says the lady, graciously
extending her hand, " and, we are told, he is
sure to appear. How odd, I was abusing you
not five minutes ago to Frank—you must have
met him as you came in,—and, behold, here you
are—not having been near me for a month ! "

" A week," answered her visitor, who always
stuck to facts. " You told me yourself one
ought never to call again at the same house
till after a decent interval. A week is decent
surely! It seems a deuced long time, I know."

"You don't suppose I've missed you," said
she, pouring out the tea. " It's all for your

own good I have you here. You'd get back to savage life again if I neglected you for a fortnight; and it *is* provoking to see all one's time and trouble thrown away! Now put your hat down, have some tea, make yourself agreeable, and you may stay for exactly three-quarters of an hour!"

To " make himself agreeable " at short notice, and to order, is a difficult task for any man. For Bill it was simply impossible. He fidgeted, gulped hot tea, and began to feel shy. She had considerable tact, however, and no little experience in the ways of young men. She neither laughed at him nor took notice of the blush he tried to keep down, but bade him throw the window open, and while he obeyed, continued carelessly, though kindly—

"In the first place, tell me all about yourself. How's Catamount ?"

She knew every one of his horses by name, and even some of the men in his troop, leading him to talk on such congenial topics with considerable ingenuity. It was this tact of hers that rendered Mrs. Lushington such a pleasant member of society, enabling her to keep her head above water deep enough to have drowned a lady with less *savoir-faire*, and consequently fewer friends.

His face brightened. "As fresh as paint!" he replied. "I beg your pardon; I mean as well as can be expected. I rode him two-and-twenty miles to-day in an hour and a half, and I give you my word when I got off him he looked as if he'd never been out of the stable."

"I should pity *you* more than your horse," she replied, with a commendable air of interest, "only I know you are never so happy as when you are trying to break your neck. You've had the grace to dress since, I see, and not badly, for once, only that handkerchief is too light a shade of blue. Now, confess! Where does she live? and is she worth riding eleven miles, there and back, to see?"

"I never know whether you're chaffing or not!" responded Bill. "You cannot believe I would gallop Catamount twenty-two miles on a hard road for any lady in the world. I don't suppose he'd take me if I wanted to go. *She*, indeed! There's no *she* in the matter!"

"You might have made *one* exception in common politeness," said Mrs. Lushington, laughing. "But I'm not satisfied yet. You and Catamount are a very flighty pair. I still .think there's a lady in the case."

"A lady in boots and spurs, then," he answered; "six foot high, with grey moustaches

and a lame leg from a sabre-cut—a lady who
has been thirty years soldiering, and never
gave or questioned an unreasonable order. Do
you know *many* ladies of that stamp, Mrs.
Lushington? I only know one, and she has
made *my* regiment the smartest in the service."

"I *do* know your Colonel a little," said she.
"I met him once at Aldershot, and though he
is anything but an old woman, I consider him
an old *dear!* So I am not very far wrong,
after all. Now, what did he want you for? Sent
for you, of course, to have—what do you call
it?—*a wigging.* I'm afraid, Master Bill, you're a
sad, bad boy, and always getting into scrapes."

"Wigging!" he repeated indignantly. "Not
a bit of it; nothing could have been kinder than
the Chief. He's the best old fellow in the
world! I wasn't sent for. I didn't go on my
own account; I went down about Daisy."

Then he stopped short, afraid of having committed himself, and conscious that at the present
crisis of his brother-officer's affairs, the less said
about them the better.

But who, since the days of Samson, was
ever able to keep a secret from a woman resolved to worm it out? As the strong man in
Delilah's lap, so was Bill in the boudoir of Mrs.
Lushington.

"Daisy," she repeated; "do you know anything of Daisy? Tell me all about him. We're
so interested, you can't think, and so sorry for
his difficulties. I wish I could help him. Is
there nothing to be done?"

Touched by her concern for his friend's wel-
fare, he trusted her at once.

"You won't mention it," said he; "Daisy
was with me at Kensington to-day. He can't
show yet, you know; but still we hope to make

it all right in time. He's got a month's leave
for the present; and I packed him off, to start
by the Irish mail to-night, just before I came to
see you. He'll keep quiet over there, and people
won't know where he is; so they can't write,
and then say he doesn't answer their letters.
Anything to put off the smash as long as possible. One can never tell what may turn up."

"You're a kind friend," she replied approvingly, "and a good boy. There! that's a great
deal for me to say. Now tell me *where* the poor
fellow is gone."

"You won't breathe it to a soul," said honest
Bill—"not even to Mr. Lushington?"

"Not even to Mr. Lushington!" she protested, greatly amused.

He gave her the address with profound
gravity, and an implicit reliance on her secrecy.

"A hill-farmer in Roscommon!" she ex-

claimed. " I know the man. His name is
Denis ; I saw him at Punchestown."

"You know everything," he said, in a tone
of admiration. " It must be very jolly to be
clever, and that."

" It's much jollier to be 'rich and that,'"
was her answer. " Money is what we all seem
to want—especially poor Daisy. Now, how
much do you suppose it would take to set him
straight ? "

He was not the man to trust any one by
halves. "Three thousand," he declared frankly;
" and where he is to get it beats me altogether.
Of course he can't hide for ever. After a time
he must come back to do duty; then there'll be a
show up, and he'll have to leave the regiment."

"And you will get your troop," said Mrs.
Lushington. " You see I know all about that
too."

His own promotion, however, as has been said, afforded this kind-hearted young gentleman no sort of consolation. ·

"I hope it won't come to that," was his comment on the military knowledge of his hostess. "I've great faith in luck. When things are at their worst, they mend. Never say die till your dead, Mrs. Lushington. Take your 'crowners' good-humouredly. Stick to your horse; and don't let go of the bridle!"

"You've been here more than your three-quarters of an hour," said Mrs. Lushington, "and you're beginning to talk slang, so you'd better depart. But you're improving, I *think*, and you may come again. Let me see, the day after to-morrow, if the Colonel don't object, and if you can find another handkerchief with a deeper shade of blue."

So Bill took his leave, and proceeded to

"The Rag," where he meant to dine in company with other choice spirits, wondering whether it would ever be his lot to marry a woman
like Mrs. Lushington—younger, of course, and
perhaps, though he hardly ventured to tell
himself so, with a little less chaff—doubting
the while if he could consent so entirely to
change his condition and his daily, or perhaps
rather his *nightly*, habits of life. He need not
give up the regiment, he reflected, and could
keep Catamount, though the stud might have
to be reduced. But what would become of
Benjamin? Was it possible any lady would
permit the badger to occupy a bottom drawer
in her wardrobe? This seemed a difficult question. Pending its solution, perhaps he had
better remain as he was!

CHAPTER XIX.

"THE RIVER'S BRIM."

DAISY was sick of the Channel. He had crossed and re-crossed it so often of late as to loathe its dancing waters, yawning in the face of Welsh and Wicklow mountains alike, wearied even of the lovely scenery that adorns the coast on either side.

He voted himself so tired in body and mind, that he must stay a day or two in Dublin to refresh.

A man who balances on the verge of ruin always has plenty of money in his pocket for immediate necessities. The expiring flame leaps up with a flash; the end of the bottle bubbles out with a gush ; and the ebbing tide of wealth leaves, here and there, a handful of loose cash on the deserted shore.

Daisy drove to the most expensive hotel in Dublin, where he ordered a capital breakfast and a comfortable room. The future seemed very uncertain. In obedience to an instinct of humanity, that bids men pause and dally with any crisis of their fate, he determined to enjoy to-day and let to-morrow take care of itself.

Nobody could be more unlikely to analyse his own sensations. It was not the practice of the regiment; but had Daisy been given to self-examination, it would have puzzled him to explain why he felt in such good humour, and so well-satisfied—buoyed up with hope, when he ought to have been sunk and overwhelmed in despair.

"Waiter," said the fugitive, while he finished his tea and ordered a glass of curaçoa. "Has Mr. Sullivan been here this morning ?"

"He *did*, sur," answered the waiter, with a pleasant grin. "Sure he brought a harse for the master to see. Five years old, Captain. A clane-bred ` one, like what ye ride yerself. There's not the aqual of him, they do be braggin', for leppin', in Westmeath, an' thim parts, up there, where he was trained."

Now Daisy wanted a horse no more than he wanted an alligator. He could neither afford to buy nor keep one, and had two or three of his own that it was indispensable to sell, yet his eye brightened, his spirits rose, with the bare possibility of a deal. He might see the animal, at any rate, he thought, perhaps ride it—there would be others probably to show; he could spend a few pleasant hours in examining their points, discussing their merits, and interchanging with Mr. Sullivan those brief and pithy remarks, intelligible only to the initiated, which he esteemed the essence of pleasant conversation. Like many other young men, Daisy was bitten with hippomania. He thoroughly enjoyed the humours of a dealer's yard. The horses interested, the owner amused him. He liked the selection, the bargaining, the running up and down, the speculation, and the slang. To use his own words—" He never could resist *the rattle of a hat !* "

It is no wonder then, that " the Captain," as Mr. Sullivan called him, spent his whole afternoon at a snug little place within an easy drive of Dublin, where that worthy, though not by way of being in the profession, inhabited a clean

white-washed house, with a few acres of marvel-
lously green paddock, and three or four loose
boxes, containing horses of various qualities,
good, bad, and indifferent. Here, after flying,
for an hour or two, over the adjoining fields and
fences, Daisy, with considerable difficulty, re-
sisted the purchase (on credit) of a worn out
black, a roan with heavy shoulders, and a
three-year-old, engaged in the following autumn
at the Curragh; but afforded their owner perfect satisfaction by the encomiums he passed
on their merits, no less than by the masterly
manner in which he handled them, at the formidable fences that bordered Mr. Sullivan's
domain.

"An' ye'll take nothing away with ye but a
fishing-rod!" said the latter, pressing on his
visitor the refreshment of whiskey, with or
without water. "Ye're welcome to't, annyhow

—more by token that ye'll bring it back again
when ye've done with it, Captain, and proud I'll
be to get another visit from ye, when ye're travelling the country, to or from Dublin, at anny
time. May be in the back end of the year I'll
have wan to show ye in thim boxes, that ye
niver seen the likes of him for lep-racin'.
Whisper now. He's bet the Black Baron in a
trial; and for Shaneen, him that wan the race
off *your* mare at Punchestown,—wait till I tell
ye,—at even weights, he'd go and *lose* little
Shaneen in two miles!"

Promising to return at a future time for in-
spection of this paragon, and disposing the
borrowed fishing-rod carefully on an outside car
he had chartered for his expedition, Daisy
returned to Dublin, ate a good dinner, drank
a bottle of dry champagne, and went to sleep
in the comfortable bedroom of his comfortable

hotel, as if he had not a care nor a debt in the world.

Towards morning, his lighter slumbers may have been visited by dreams, and if so, it is probable that fancy clothed her visions in a similitude of Norah Macormac. Certainly, his first thought on waking was for that young lady, as his opening eyes rested on the fishing-rod, which he had borrowed chiefly on her account.

In truth, Daisy felt inclined to put off as long as possible the exile—for he could think of it in no more favourable light—that he had brought on himself in the Roscommon mountains.

Mr. Sullivan, when the sport of fly-fishing came in his way, was no mean disciple of the gentle art. Observing a salmon-rod in that worthy's sitting-room, of which apartment, indeed, with two foxes'-brushes and a baro-meter, it constituted the principal furniture,

Daisy bethought him, that on one of his visits
to Cormac's-town, its hospitable owner had given
him leave and license to fish the Dabble whenever he pleased, whether staying at the Castle
or not. The skies were cloudy—as usual in
Ireland, there was no lack of rain—surely, this
would be a proper occasion to take advantage
of Macormac's kindness, protract his stay in
Dublin, and run down daily by the train to fish,
so long as favourable weather lasted, and his
own funds held out.

We are mostly self-deceivers, though there
exists something *within* each of us that is not to
be hoodwinked nor imposed upon by the most
specious of fallacies.

It is probable Daisy never confessed to himself how the fish he *really* wanted to angle for
was already more than half-hooked ; how it was
less the attraction of a salmon than a mermaid

that drew him to the margin of the Dabble; and, how he cared very little that the sun shone bright or the river waned, so as he might but hear the light step of Norah Macormac on the shingle, look in the fair face that turned so pale and sad when he went away, that would smile and blush its welcome so kindly when he came again.

He must have loved her without knowing it; and perhaps such insensible attachments, waxing stronger day by day, strike the deepest root, and boast the longest existence—hardy plants that live and flourish through the frowns of many winters, contrasting nobly with more brilliant and ephemeral posies, forced by circumstances to sudden maturity and rapid decay—

> " As flowers that first in spring-time burst,
> The earliest wither too."

Nevertheless, for both sexes—

VOL. II.   F

"'Tis all but a dream at the best: "

and Norah Macormac's vision, scarcely acknow-
ledged while everything went smoothly, assumed very glowing colours when the impossi-
bility of its realisation dawned on her, and Lady
Mary pointed out the folly of an attachment to a
penniless subaltern, unsteady in habits, while
addicted overmuch to sports of the field.

With average experience and plenty of common-sense, the mother had been sorely puzzled
how to act. She was well aware that advice in
such cases, however judiciously administered,
often irritates the wound it is intended to heal;
that "warnings" — to use her own words —
"only put things in people's heads; " and that a
fancy, like a heresy, sometimes dies out un-
noticed, when it is not to be stifled by argument
nor extirpated with the strong hand. Yet
how might she suffer this pernicious supersti-

tion to grow, under her very eyes? Was she
not a woman, and must she not speak her
mind? Besides, she blamed her own blindness,
that her daughter's intimacy with the scape-
grace had been unchecked in its commence-
ment, and, smarting with self-reproach, could
not forbear crying aloud, when she had better
have held her tongue!

So Miss Norah discovered she was in love,
after all. Mamma said so; no doubt mamma
was right. The young lady had herself suspected something of the kind long ago, but
Lady Mary's authority and remonstrances
placed the matter beyond question. She was
very fond of her mother, and, to do her justice,
tried hard to follow her ladyship's advice. So
she thought the subject over, day by day,
argued it on every side, in accordance with,
in opposition to, and independent of, her own

inclinations, to find as a result, that during waking and sleeping hours alike, the image of Daisy was never absent from her mind.

Then a new beauty seemed to dawn in the sweet young face. The very peasants about the place noticed a change; little Ella, playing at being grown-up, pretended she was "Sister Norah going to be married;" and papa, when she retired with her candle at night, turning fondly to his wife, would declare—

"She'll be the pick of the family now, mamma, when all's said and done! They're a fair-looking lot, even the boys. Divil thank them, then, on the mother's side! But it's Norah that's likest yourself, my dear, when we were young, only not quite so stout, maybe, and a thought less colour in her cheek."

Disturbed at the suggestion, while gratified by the compliment, Lady Mary, in a fuss of

increased anxiety, felt fonder than ever of her
child. In Norah's habits also there came an
alteration, as in her countenance. She sat
much in the library, with a book on her knee,
of which she seldom turned the page ; played
long *solos* on the pianoforte, usually while the
others were out; went to bed early, but lay
awake for hours ; rode very little, and walked
a great deal, though the walks were often
solitary, and almost invariably in the direction
of a certain waterfall, to which she had
formerly conducted Miss Douglas, while showing off to her new friend the romantic beauties
of the Dabble.

The first day Mr. Walters put his borrowed
rod together on the banks of this pretty stream
it rained persistently in a misty drizzle, borne
on the soft south wind. He killed an eight-
pound fish, yet returned to Dublin in an un-

accountable state of disappointment, not to say disgust. He got better after dinner, and, with another bottle of dry champagne, determined to try again.

The following morning rose in unclouded splendour—clear blue sky, blazing sun, and not a breath of wind. A more propitious day could scarcely be imagined for a cricket-match, an archery-meeting, or a picnic; but in such weather the crafty angler leaves rod and basket at home. Daisy felt a little ashamed of these paraphernalia in the train, but proceeded to the water-side nevertheless, and prepared deliberately for his task, looking up and down the stream meanwhile with considerable anxiety.

All at once he felt his heart beating fast, and began to flog the water with ludicrous assiduity.

It is difficult to explain the gentleman's perturbation (for why was he there at all?), though the lady's astonishment can easily be accounted for, when Norah, thinking of him every moment, and visiting this particular spot only because it reminded her of his presence, found herself, at a turn in the river, not ten paces from the man whom, a moment before, she feared she was never to see again!

Yet did she remain outwardly the more composed of the two, and was first to speak.

"Daisy!" she exclaimed—"Captain Walters —I never thought you were still in Ireland. You'll be coming to the Castle to dinner, anyhow."

He blushed, he stammered, he looked like a fool (though Norah didn't think so), he got out with difficulty certain incoherent sentences about "fishing," and "flies," and "liberty from your father," and lastly, recovering a little, "the ten-pounder *I* rose and *you* landed, by the black stump there, under the willow."

As he regained his confidence, she lost hers—almost wishing she hadn't come, or had put her veil down, or she didn't exactly know what. In a trembling voice, and twining her fingers nervously together, she propounded the pertinent question—

"How—how did you find your brother-officers when you got back to the regiment?"

Its absurdity struck them both. Simultaneously they burst out laughing: their reserve vanished from that moment. He took both her hands in his, and the rod lay neglected on the shingle, while he exclaimed—

"I *am* so pleased to see you again! Miss Macormac—Norah! I fished here all yesterday, hoping you'd come. I'm glad, though, you didn't; you'd have got such a wetting."

"Did you now?" was her answer, while the beautiful grey eyes deepened, and the blood mantled in her cheek. "Indeed, then, it's for little I'd have counted the wetting, if I'd only known. But how *was* I to know, Captain Walters—well, Daisy, then—that you'd be shooting up the river, like a young salmon, only to see *me?* And supposing I *had* known it, or thought it, or wished it even, I'm afraid I ought never to have come."

"But now you *are* here," argued Daisy, with some show of reason, "you'll speak to me, won't you? and help me to fish, and let me walk back with you part of the way home?"

It seemed an impotent conclusion, but she was in no mood to be censorious.

"I'm very pleased to see you, and that's the truth," she answered; "but as for fishing, I'll

engage ye'll never rise a fish in the Dabble
with a sky like that. I'll stay just five minutes,
though, while ye wet your line, anyhow. Oh!
Daisy, don't you remember what a trouble we
had with the big fish down yonder, the time
I ran to fetch the gaff?"

"Remember!" said Daisy, "I should think
I *do !* How quick you were about it. I didn't
think any girl in the world could run so fast.
I can remember everything you've said and
done since I've known you. That's the worst
of it, Norah. It's got to be different after to-
day."

She had been laughing and blushing at his
recollections of her activity; but she glanced
quickly in his face now, while her own turned
very grave and pale.

"Ye're coming to the Castle, of course,"
said she. "I'll run home this minute, and tell

mamma to order a room, and we'll send the
car round to the station for your things."

She spoke in hurried, nervous accents, dread-
ing to hear what was coming, yet conscious
she had never felt so happy in her life.

Formerly she considered Daisy the lightest-
hearted of men. Hitherto she scarcely remembered to have seen a cloud on his face.
She liked it none the worse for its gravity
now.

"I've been very unlucky, Norah," said he,
holding her hand, and looking thoughtfully on
the river as it flowed by. "Perhaps it's my
own fault. I shall never visit at Cormac's-town,
nor go into any society where I've a chance of
meeting *you* again. And yet I've done nothing
wrong nor disgraceful as yet."

"I knew it!" she exclaimed; "I'd have
sworn it on the Book! I told mamma so.

He's a *gentleman,* I said, and that's enough for me !' "

" Thank you, dear," answered Daisy, in a failing voice. " I'm glad *you* didn't turn against me. It's bad enough without that."

" But what *has* happened ?" she asked, drawing closer to his side. " Couldn't any of us help you ? Couldn't papa advise you what to do ?"

" *This* has happened, Norah," he answered gravely. " I am completely ruined. I have got nothing left in the world. Worse still, I am afraid I can scarce pay up all I've lost."

The spirit of her ancestors came into her eyes and bearing. Ruin to these, like personal danger, had never seemed a matter of great moment, so long as, at any sacrifice, honour might be preserved. She raised her head proudly, and looked straight in his face.

"The last *must* be done," said she. "*Must* be done, I'm telling you, Daisy, and *shall* be, if we sell the boots, you and me, off our very feet! How near can you get to what you owe for wagers and things? Of course, they'll have to be paid the first."

"If *everything* goes, I don't see my way to pay up all," he answered. "However, they *must* give me a little time. Where I'm to go, though, or what to do, is more than I can tell. But Norah, dear Norah! what I mind most is, that I musn't hope to see *you* again!"

Her tears were falling fast. Her hands were busy with a locket she wore round her neck, the only article of value Norah possessed in the world. But the poor fingers trembled so, they failed to undo the strip of velvet on which it hung. At last she got it loose, and

pressed it into his hand. "Take it, Daisy,"
said she, smiling with her wet eyes; "I don't
value it a morsel. It was old Aunt Macormac
gave it me on my birth-day. There's diamonds
in it—not Irish, dear—and its worth something,
anyway, though not much. Ah, Daisy! now,
if ye won't take it, I'll think ye never cared
for me one bit!"

But Daisy stoutly refused to despoil her of
this keepsake, though he begged hard, of
course, for the velvet ribbon to which it was
attached; and those who have ever found
themselves in a like situation, will understand
that he did not ask in vain.

So Miss Macormac returned to the Castle
and the maternal wing, too late for luncheon;
but thus far engaged to her ruined admirer,
that while he vowed to come back the very
moment his prospects brightened, and the

" something " turned up which we all expect but so few of us experience—she promised, on her part, " never to marry (how could you think it now, Daisy!) nor so much as look at anybody else till she saw him again, if it wasn't for a hundred years ! "

I am concerned to add that Mr. Sullivan's rod remained forgotten on the shingle, where it was eventually picked up by one of Mr. Macormac's keepers, but handled by its rightful owner no more. There was nothing to keep Daisy in Dublin now, and his funds were getting low. In less than twenty-four hours from his parting with Norah Macormac, he found himself crossing that wild district of Roscommon where he had bought the famous black mare that had so influenced his fortunes. Toiling, on an outside car, up the long ascent that led to the farmer's house, he could scarcely believe so short a time had elapsed since he visited the same place in the flush of youth and hope. He felt quite old and broken by compar son. Years count for little compared to events; and age is more a question of experience than of time. He had one consolation, however, and it lay in the shape of a narrow velvet ribbon next his heart.

Ere he had clasped the farmer's hand at his own gate, and heard his cheery, hospitable greeting, he wondered how he could feel so happy.

"I'm proud to see ye, Captain!" said Denis, flourishing his hat round his head, as if it was a slip of blackthorn. "Proud am I an' pleased to see ye back again—an' that's the truth! Ye're welcome, I tell ye! Step in, now, an' take something at wanst. See, Captain, there's a two-year-old in that stable; the very moral of your black mare. Ye never seen her likes for leppin'! Ye'll try the baste this very afternoon, with the blessin'. I've had th' ould saddle mended, an' the stirrups altered to your length."

CHAPTER XX.

TAKING THE COLLAR.

THE General thought he had never been so happy in his life. His voice, his bearing, his very dress seemed to partake of the delusion that gilded existence. Springing down the steps of his Club, with more waist in his coat, more pretension in his hat, more agility in his gait than was considered usual, or even decorous, amongst its frequenters, no wonder they passed their comments freely enough on their old comrade, ridiculing or deploring his fate, according to the various opinions and temper of the conclave.

"What's up with St. Josephs now?" asked a white-whiskered veteran of his neighbour, whose bluff, weather-beaten face proclaimed him an Admiral of the Red. "He's turned quite flighty and queer of late. Nothing wrong *here*, is there?" and the speaker pointed a shaking finger to the apex of his own bald head.

"Not *there*, but *here*," answered the sailor, laying his remaining arm across his breast. "Going to be spliced, they tell me. Sorry for it. He's not a bad sort; and a smartish officer as I've heard, in *your* service."

"Pretty well—so, so. Nothing extraordinary for *that*," answered the first speaker, commonly called by irreverent juniors "Old Straps." "He hadn't much to do in India, I fancy; but he's been lucky, sir, lucky, and luck's the thing! Luck against the world, Admiral, by sea or land!"

"Well, his luck's over now, it seems," grunted the Admiral, whose views on matrimony appeared to differ from those of his profession in general. "I'm told he's been fairly hooked by that Miss Douglas. Black-eyed girl, with black hair—black, and all black, d—me!—and rides a black mare in the park. Hey! Why, she might be his daughter. How d'ye mean?"

"More fool he," replied Straps, with a leer and a grin that disclosed his yellow tusks. "A fellow like St. Josephs ought to know better."

"I'm not so sure of that," growled the Admiral. "Gad, sir, if I was idiot enough to do the same thing, d'ye think I'd take a d—d old catamaran, that knew every move in the game? No, no, sir; youth and innocence, hey? A clean bill of health, a fair wind, and a pleasant voyage, you know!"

"In my opinion, there's devilish little youth

left, and no innocence," answered "Straps." "If that's the girl, she's been hawked about, to my certain knowledge, for the last three seasons ; and I suppose our friend is the only chance left—what we used to call a 'forlorn hope' when I was an ensign. He's got a little money, and they might give him a command. You never know what this Government will do. It's my belief they'd give that crossing-sweeper a command if they were only sure he was quite unfit for it."

"Command be d——d!" swore the Admiral. "He'll have enough to do to command his young wife. What? She's a lively craft, I'll be bound, with her black eyes. Carries a weather-helm, and steers as wild as you please in a sea-way. I'll tell you what it is—— Here, waiter! bring me the *Globe.* Why the ——are the evening papers so late?"

In the rush for those welcome journals, so
long expected, so eagerly seized, all other
topics were instantaneously submerged. Long
before he could reach the end of the street,
General St. Josephs was utterly forgotten by
his brother officers and friends.

Still he *thought* he had never been so happy
in his life. The word is used advisedly ; for
surely experience teaches us that real happiness consists in tranquillity and repose, in the
slumber rather than the dream, in the lassitude
that soothes the patient, not the fever-fit of
which it is the result. Can a man be considered happy who is not comfortable ? and
how is comfort compatible with "anxiety, loss
of appetite, nervous tremors, giddiness, in-
voluntary blushing," and the many symptoms
of disorder, which could be cured heretofore
by advertisement, and which are the invariable

accompaniments of an epidemic, invincible by pill or potion, and yielding only to the homœopathic treatment of marriage.

In this desperate remedy St. Josephs was anxious to experimentalise, and without delay. Yet his tact was supreme. Since the memorable walk in Kensington Gardens, when he had laid her under such heavy obligations, his demeanour had been more that of a friend than a lover—more, perhaps, that of a loyal and devoted subject to his sovereign mistress than either. She wondered why he never asked her, what she had done with all that money? Why, when she alluded to the subject, he winced and started as from a touch on a raw wound. Once she very nearly told him all. They were in a box at the Opera, so far unobserved that the couple who had accompanied them seemed wholly engrossed with each other.

Satanella longed to make her confession—ease her conscience of its burden, perhaps, though such a thought was cruel and unjust—shake the yoke from off her neck. She had even got as far as, " I've never half thanked you, General——" when there came a tap at the box-door. Enter an irreproachable dandy, then a confusion of tongues, a laugh, a solo, injunctions to silence, and the opportunity was gone! Could she ever find courage to seek for it again ?

Nevertheless, day by day she dwelt more on her admirer's forbearance, his care, his tenderness, his chivalrous devotion. Though he never pressed the point, it seemed an understood thing that they were engaged. She had forbidden him to visit her before luncheon, but he spent his afternoons in her drawing-room; and, on rare occasions, was admitted

in the evening, when an elderly lady, supposed
to be Blanche's cousin, came to act chaperone.
The walks in Kensington Gardens had been
discontinued. Her heart could not but smite
her sometimes, to think that she never gave
him but that one, when she wanted him to do
her a favour.

Had he been more exacting she would have
felt less self-reproach, but his patience and
good humour cut her to the quick.

"You brute!" she would say, pushing her
hair back, and frowning at her own handsome
face in the glass. "You *worse* than brute!—
unfeeling, unfeminine. I wish you were dead!
—I wish you were dead!"

She had lost her rich colour now, and the
hollow eyes were beginning to look very large
and sad, under their black arching brows.

Perhaps it was the General's greatest delight

to hear her sing. This indulgence she accorded him only of an evening, when the cousin invariably went to sleep, and her admirer sat in an arm-chair with the daily paper before his face. She insisted on this screen, and this attitude, never permitting him to stand by the pianoforte, nor turn over the leaves, nor undergo any exertion of mind or body that should break the charm. Who knows what golden visions gladdened the war-worn soldier's heart while he leaned back and listened, spell-bound by the tones he loved? Dreams of domestic happiness and peaceful joys, and a calm, untroubled future, when doubts and fears should be over, and he could make this glorious creature wholly and exclusively his own.

Did he ever wonder why in certain songs the dear voice thrilled with a sweetness akin to pain, ere it was drowned in a loud and brilliant accompaniment, that foiled the possibility of remonstrance, while the ditty was thrown aside to be replaced by another, less fraught, perhaps, with trying memories and associations? If so, he hazarded no remark nor conjecture, satisfied, as it seemed, to wait her pleasure, and in all things bow his will to hers, sacrificing his desires, his pride, his very self-respect to the woman he adored.

For a time nothing occurred to disturb the General's enforced tranquillity, and he pursued the course he seemed to have marked out for himself with a calm perseverance that deserved success. In public, people glanced and whispered when they saw Miss Douglas on his arm; in private, he called daily at her house, talked much small-talk, and drank a great deal of weak tea; while in solitude he asked himself how long this probation was to last, resolving nevertheless to curb his impatience, control his temper, and if the prize was only to be won by waiting, wait for it to the end!

Leaving his Club, then, unconscious of the Admiral's pity and the sarcasms of "Old Straps," St. Josephs walked jauntily through Mayfair, till he came to the well-known street, which seemed to him now even as a glade in Paradise. The crossing-sweeper blessed him with considerable emphasis, brushing energetically in his path; for when going the General was invariably good for sixpence, and on propitious days would add thereto a shilling as he returned.

On the present occasion, though his hand was in his pocket, it remained there with the coin in its finger and thumb; for the wayfarer stopped petrified in the middle of the street; the sweeper held his tattered hat at arm's-length, motionless as a statue; and a bare-headed butcher's-boy, standing erect in a light cart, pulled his horse on its haunches, and called out—

"Now then, stoopid! d'ye want all the road to yerself?" grazing the old officer's coat-tails as he drove by with a brutal laugh.

But neither irreverence nor outrage served to divert the General's attention from the sight that so disturbed his equanimity.

"There's that d——d black mare again!" he muttered, while he clenched his teeth, and his cheek turned pale. "I'll put a stop to this one way or the other. Steady, steady! No; my game is to be won by pluck and patience. It's very near the end now. Shall I lose it by failing in both?"

The black mare, looking but little the worse for training, was indeed in the act of leaving

Blanche's door. Miss Douglas had evidently ridden her that morning in the Park. She might have told the General, he thought. She might have asked him to accompany her as he used. She ought to have no secrets from him now; but was he in truth any nearer her inner life, any more familiar with her dearest thoughts and wishes than he had been months ago? Surely she was not treating him well! Surely he deserved more confidence than this. The General felt very sore and angry; but summoning all his self-command, walked up-stairs, —and for this he deserves no little credit,—with an assured step, and a calm, unruffled brow.

"Miss Douglas was dressing," the servant said. "Miss Douglas had been out for a ride. Would the General take a seat, and look at to-day's paper? Miss Douglas had said '*par-tic'lar*' she would be at home."

It was irritating to wait, but it was soothing to know she was at home "*partic'lar*" when *he* called. The General sat down to peruse the advertisement sheet of the paper, reading absently a long and laudatory description of the trousseaux and other articles for family use supplied by a certain house in the City at less than cost price!

CHAPTER XXI.

A SNAKE IN THE GRASS.

HIS studies were soon interrupted by the rustle of a dress on the staircase. With difficulty he forbore from rushing out to meet its wearer, but managed to preserve the composure of an ordinary morning visitor, when the door opened, and—enter Mrs. Lushington!

She must have read his disappointment in his face; for she looked half-amused, half-provoked, and there was no less malice than mirth in her eyes while she observed—

"Blanche will be down directly, General, and

don't be afraid I shall interrupt your *tête-à-tête*, for I am going away as soon as I've written a note. You can rehearse all the charming things you have got to say in the meantime."

He had recovered his *savoir-faire*.

"Rehearse them to *you* ?" he asked, laughing. "It would be pretty practice, no doubt. Shall I begin ?"

"Not now," she answered, in the same tone. "There is hardly time ; though Blanche wouldn't be very cross about it, I dare say. She is liberal enough, and knows she can trust *me*."

"I am sure you are a true friend," he returned gravely. "Miss Douglas—Blanche—has not too many. I hope you will always remain one of her staunchest and best."

She smiled sadly.

"Do you *really* mean it ?" said she, taking

his hand. " You can't imagine how happy it makes me to hear you say so. I thought you considered me a vain, ignorant, frivolous little woman, like the rest."

Perhaps he did, but this was not the moment to confess it.

" What a strange world it would be," he answered, " if we 'knew the real opinions of our friends. In this case, Mrs. Lushington, you see how wrong you were about mine."

" I believe you, General ! " she exclaimed. " I feel that you are truth itself. I am sure you never deceived a woman in your life, and I *cannot* understand how any woman could find it in her heart to deceive *you*. One ought never to forgive such an offence, and I can believe that *you* never would."

He thought her earnestness unaccountable, and wholly uncalled for; but his senses were on the alert to catch the first symptoms of Blanche's approach, and he answered rather absently—

"Quite right! Of course not. Double-dealing is *the* thing I hate. You may cheat me once; that is *your* fault. It is my own if you ever take me in again."

"No wonder Blanche values your good opinion," said Mrs. Lushington meaningly. "She has not spent her life amongst people whose standard is so high. Hush! here she comes. Ah! General, you won't care about talking to *me* now!"

She gave him one reproachful glance in which there was a little merriment, a little pique, and a great deal of tender interest, ere she departed to write her note in the back drawing-room.

It was impossible not to contrast her kind and deferential manner with the cold, collected bearing of Miss Douglas, who entered the room, like a queen about to hold her court, rather than a loving maiden, hurrying to meet her lord.

She had always been remarkable for quiet dignity, in motion or repose.

It was one of the many charms on which the General lavished his admiration, but he could have dispensed with this royal composure now. It seemed a little out of place in their relative positions. Also, he would have liked to see the colour deepen in her proud, impassive face, though his honest heart ached while he reflected how the bright tints had faded of late, how the glory of her beauty had departed, leaving her always pale and saddened now.

He would have asked a leading question, hazarded a gentle reproach, or in some way made allusion to the arrival of his *bête noir*, but her altered looks disarmed him; and it was

Satanella herself who broached the subject, by quietly informing her visitor she had just returned from riding the black mare in the Park. " Do you *mind ? "* she added, rising in some confusion to pull a blind down, while she spoke.

Here would have been an opportunity for a confession of jealousy, an appeal to her feelings, pleadings, promises, protestations,—to use the General's own metaphor,—" an attack along the whole line ; " but how was he thus to offer battle, with his flank exposed and threatened, with Mrs. Lushington's ears wide open and attentive, while her pen went scribble, scribble, almost in the same room ?

" I *mind* everything you do," said he gallantly, " and object to nothing ! If I *did* want to get up a grievance, I should quarrel with you for not ordering me to parade in attendance on you in the Park. My time, as you know, is always yours, and I am never so happy as with you. Blanche "—(dropping his voice)—"I am never *really* happy when you are out of my sight."

She glanced towards the writing-table, and though the folding doors, half-shut, concealed that lady's person, seemed glad to observe, by the continual scratching of a pen, that Mrs. Lushington had not yet finished her note.

" You are always good and kind," said Blanche, forcing a smile. " Far more than I deserve. Will you ride another day, early ? Thanks ; I knew you would. I should have asked you this morning, but I had a head-ache, and thought I should only be a bore. Besides, I expected you in the afternoon. Then Clara came to luncheon, and we went up-stairs, and now the carriage will be round in five minutes. That is the way the day goes by ; yet it seems very long too, only not so bad as the night."

Again his face fell. It was up-hill work, he thought. Surely women were not usually so difficult to woo, or his own memory played him false, and his friends romanced unpardonably in their narratives. But, nevertheless, in all the prizes of life that which seemed fairest and best hung highest out of reach, and he would persevere to the end. Ay! even if he should fail at last!

Miss Douglas seemed to possess some intuitive knowledge of his intention, and conscious of his determination to overcome them, was perhaps the more disposed to throw difficulties in his path. He should have remembered that in love as in war, a rapid flank movement and complete change of tactics will often prevail, when vigilance, endurance, and honest courage have been tried in vain.

Satanella could not but appreciate a delicacy

that forbade further inquiry about the black
mare. No sooner had she given vent to her
feelings, in the little explosion recorded above,
than she bitterly regretted their expression,
comparing her wayward, petulant disposition
with the temper and constancy displayed by her
admirer. Sorrowful, softened, filled with self-
reproach, she gave him one of her winning
smiles, and bade him forgive her display of ill-
humour, or bear with it, as one of many evil
qualities, the result of her morbid temperament
and isolated lot.

"Then I slept badly, and went out tired. The
Ride was crowded, the sun broiling, the mare
disagreeable. Altogether, I came back as cross
as two sticks. General, are *you* never out of
humour? And how do you get rid of your ill-
tempers? You certainly don't visit them on
me !"

" How *could* I ?" he asked in return. " How can I ever be anything but your servant, your slave ? Oh ! Blanche, you must believe me *now*. How much longer is my probation to last ? Is the time to be always put off from day to day, and must I——"

"Clara ! Clara !" exclaimed Miss Douglas to her friend in the back drawing-room, " shall you never have done with those tiresome letters ? Have you any idea what o'clock it is ? And the carriage was ordered at five ! "

The General smothered a curse. It was invariably so. No sooner did he think he had gained a secure footing, wrested a position of advantage, than she cut the ground from under him, pushed him down the hill, and his labour was lost, his task all to begin again ! It seemed as if she could not bear to face her real position, glancing off at a tangent, without the slightest compunction, from the one important topic he was constantly watching an opportunity to broach.

"Just done! and a good day's work too!" replied Mrs. Lushington's silver tones from the writing-table, and it must have been a quicker ear than either Satanella's or the General's to detect in that playful sentence the spirit of mischievous triumph it conveyed.

Mrs. Lushington was delighted. She felt sure she had fathomed a secret, discovered the clue to an intrigue, and by such means as seemed perfectly fair and justifiable to her warped sense of right and wrong.

Finding herself the third person in a small party that should have been limited to two, she made urgent correspondence her excuse for withdrawing to such a distance as might admit of overhearing their conversation, while the lovers, if lovers indeed they were, should think themselves unobserved.

So she opened Satanella's blotting-book, and spread a sheet of note-paper on its folds.

Mrs. Lushington had a quick eye, no less than a ready wit. Blanche's blotting-paper was of the best quality, soft, thick, and absorbent. Where the writing-book opened, so shrewd an observer did not fail to detect the words " Roscommon, Ireland," traced clear and distinct as a lithograph, though reversed. Looking through the page, against the light, she read Daisy's address in his hiding-place with his humble friend Denis, plainly enough, and the one word " Registered" underlined at the corner.

" *Enfin je te pince !* " she muttered below her breath. It was evident Satanella was in Daisy's confidence, that she knew his address,—which had been extorted indeed with infinite trouble from a lad whom he sent to England in charge of the precious mare,—and had written to him within the last day or two. It was a great discovery! Her hand shook from sheer excitement, while she considered how best it could be turned to account, how it might serve to wean the General of his infatuation, to detach him from her friend, perhaps at last to secure him for herself. But she must proceed cautiously; make every step good as she went on; prove each link of the chain while she forged it; and when Blanche was fairly in the toils, show her the usual mercy extended by one woman to another.

Of course, she wrote her notes on a fresh page of the blotting-book. Of course, she rose from her employment frank, smiling, unsuspicious. Of course, she was more than usually affectionate to Blanche; and that young lady, well-skilled in the wiles of her own sex, wondering what had happened, watched her friend's conduct with some anxiety and yet more contempt.

"Good-bye, Blanche."

"Good-bye, Clara."

"Come again soon, dear!"

"You may depend upon me, love!"

And they kissed each other with a warmth of affection in no way damped or modified because Blanche suspected, and Clara resolved, henceforth it must be war to the knife!

In taking her leave of the General, however, Mrs. Lushington could not resist an allusion to their previous conversation, putting into her manner so much of tender regard and respectful interest as was pleasing enough to him and inexpressibly galling to her friend.

"Have you said your say?" she asked,

looking very pretty and good-humoured as she gave him both hands. " I'm sure you had lots of time, and the best of opportunities. Don't you think I'm very considerate?"

" More—very generous!"

" Come and see me soon. Whenever you like. With or without dear Blanche. She won't mind; I'm always at home, to either of you—or both."

Then she made a funny little courtesy, gave him one more smile, one sidelong sorrowful glance, with her hand on the door, and was gone.

Blanche's spirit rose to arms; every instinct of her sex urged her to resist this unconscionable freebooter, this lawless professor of piracy and annexation. After all, whether she cared for him or not, the General was her own property. And what right had this woman to come between mistress and servant, with her becks and leers, her smiles and wiles, and meretricious ways? She had never valued her lover higher than at the moment Mrs. Lushington left the room; but he destroyed his advantage, kicked down all his good fortune, by looking in Miss Douglas's face with an expression of slavish devotion, while he exclaimed—

"How different that woman is from you, Blanche. Surely, my queen, there is nobody like you in the world!"

CHAPTER XXII.

AN EXPERT.

RETURNING from morning stables to his barrack-room, Soldier Bill found on his table a document that puzzled him exceedingly. He read it a dozen times, turned it upside down, smoothed it out with his riding-whip, all in vain. He could make nothing of it; then he summoned Barney.

" When did this thing come, and who brought it ?"

" Five minutes back," answered the bâtman. " Left by a young man on fatigue duty."

So Barney, with military exactitude, described a government official, in the costume of its telegraphic department.

" Did the man leave no message?" continued Bill.

" Said as there was nothing to pay," answered Barney, standing at " attention," and obviously considering this part of his communication satisfactory in the extreme.

" Said there was nothing to pay!" mused his master, " and I would have given him a guinea to explain any two words of it." Then he took his coat off, and sat doggedly down to read the mysterious sentences again and again.

The soldier, as he expressed it, was "up a tree!" From its mode of transmission, he argued that the message must be of importance. The sender's name was legible enough, and his own address perfectly correct. He felt sure

Daisy would not have telegraphed from the wilds of Roscommon, but on a matter of urgency; and it did seem provoking that the only sense to be got out of the whole composition was in the sentence with which it concluded— "Do not lose a moment." In his perplexity, he could think of no one so likely to help him as Mrs. Lushington.

"She has more 'nous' in that pretty little head of hers," thought Bill, as he plunged into a suit of plain clothes, "than the Horse Guards and the War Office put together. *She'll* knock the marrow out of this, if anybody can! I've heard her guess riddles right off, the first time she heard them; and there isn't her equal in London for acting charades and games of that kind, where you must be down to it before they can say 'knife.' By Jove, I shouldn't wonder if this was a double acrostic after all! Only

Daisy wouldn't be such a flat as to telegraph it all the way from Ireland to *me*. I hope she'll see me. It's awfully early. I wonder if she'll blow me up for coming so soon."

These reflections, and Catamount's thorough-bred canter, soon brought him to Mrs. Lushington's door. She was at home, and sufficiently well prepared for exercises of ingenuity, having been engaged, after breakfast,—though it is but fair to say such skirmishes were of unusual occurrence,—in a passage-of-arms with Frank.

The latter was a good-*natured* man with a bad *temper*. His wife's temper was excellent; but her enemies, and indeed her friends, said she was ill-*natured*. Though scarcely to be called an attached couple, these two seldom found it worth while to quarrel, and so long as the selfishness of each did not clash with the other,

they jogged on quietly enough. It was only
when domestic affairs threw them together
more than common that the contact elicited
certain sparks, such as crackled on occasion
into what observers below-stairs called a "flare-
up."

To day they happened to breakfast together.
After a few "back-handers," and some rapid
exchanges, in which the husband came by the
worst, their conversation turned on money-
matters—always a sore subject, as each considered that the other spent more than a due
share of their joint income. Complaints led to
recriminations, until at length, goaded by the
sharpness of his wife's tongue, Mr. Lushington
exclaimed—"Narrow-minded, indeed! Paltry
economy! I can tell you, if I didn't keep a
precious tight hand, and deny myself—well—
lots of things. I say if I didn't deny myself

lots of things, I should be in the Bench—that's all!"

"Then you are a very bad financier," she retorted; "worse than the Chancellor of the Exchequer. But I don't believe it. I believe you're saving money every day."

He rose from his chair in a transport of irritation, the skirts of his dressing-gown floating round him like the rags of a whirling dervish.

"Saving money!" he repeated, in a sort of suppressed scream. "I can only tell you I had to borrow five-hundred last week, and from little Sharon too. That doesn't mean getting it at three per cent.!"

"Then you ought to be ashamed of yourself!" said she. "No gentleman borrows money from Sharon."

"No gentleman!" he vociferated. "Upon

my life, Mrs. Lushington, I wish you would try
to be more temperate in your language. No
gentleman, indeed! I should like to know what
you call General St. Josephs? I fancy he is
rather a favourite of yours. All I can tell you
is, *he* borrows money of Sharon. Lumps of
money, at exorbitant interest."

"It's very easy to *say* these things," she
replied. " But you can't prove them!"

"Can't I?" was his rejoinder. "Well, I
suppose you won't doubt my word when I give
you my honour, that he consulted me himself
about a loan from this very man. Three thousand pounds, Mrs. Lushington—three thousand
pounds sterling, and at two days' notice. Didn't
care what he paid for it, and wanted it—Well,
I didn't ask him why he wanted it—*I* don't pry
into other people's money-matters. *I* don't
always think the worst of my neighbours. But

you'll allow I'm right, I hope. You'll admit so much, at any rate."

"That has nothing to do with it," replied his wife; and in this highly satisfactory manner their matrimonial bicker terminated.

Mrs. Lushington, while remaining, in a modified sense, mistress of the position—for Frank retired to his own den, when the servants came to take away breakfast—found her curiosity keenly stimulated by the little piece of gossip thus let fall under the excitement of a conjugal wrangle. What on earth could St. Josephs want with three thousand pounds? She had never heard he was a gambler. On a race-course, she knew, from personal observation, that beyond a few half-crowns with the ladies, he would not venture a shilling. He had told her repeatedly how he abhorred foreign loans, joint-stock companies, lucrative investments of all sorts, and money speculations of any kind whatever; yet here, if she believed her husband, was this wise and cautious veteran plunging overhead in a transaction wholly out of keeping with his character and habits. "There *must* be a woman at the bottom of it!" thought Mrs. Lushington, not unreasonably, resolving at the same time never to rest till she had sifted the whole mystery from beginning to end.

She felt so keen on her quest, that she could even have found it in her heart to seek Frank in his own snuggery, and, sinking her dignity, there endeavour to worm out of him further particulars, when Catamount was pulled up with some difficulty at her door, and his master's card sent in, accompanied by a humble petition that the early visitor might be admitted. Having darkened her eye-lashes just before breakfast, and being, moreover, dressed in an unusually becoming morning toilet, she returned a favourable answer, so that Soldier Bill, glowing from his ride, was ushered into her boudoir without delay.

Her womanly tact observed his fussed and anxious looks. She assumed, therefore, an air of interest and gravity in her own.

"There's some bother," said she kindly; "I see it in your face. How can I help you, and what can I do?"

"You're a conjuror, by Jove!" gasped Bill, in a paroxysm of admiration at her omniscience.

"*You're* not, at any rate!" she replied, smiling. "But, come, tell me all about it. You're in a scrape? You've been a naughty boy. What have you been doing? Out with it!"

"It's nothing of my own; I give you my honour," replied Bill. "It's Daisy's turn now.

Look here, Mrs. Lushington. I'm completely
puzzled—regularly knocked out of time. Read
that. I can't make head or tail of it."

He handed her the telegram, which she
perused in silence, then burst out laughing, and
read it again aloud for his edification :—

" *Very strong Honey just arrived—bulls a-light
on Bank of Ireland — Sent by an unknown
Fiend—fail immediately — Sell Chief—consult a
Gent, and strip Aaron at once—Do not lose a
moment.*"

" Mr. Walters must be gone raving mad, or is
this a practical joke ? and why do you bring it
here ? "

" I don't think it's a joke," answered Bill
ruefully. " I brought it because you know
everything. If *you* can't help me, I'm done ! "

" Quite right," said she. " Always consult a
woman in a tangle. Now this thing is just

like a skein of silk. If we can't unravel it at one end, we begin at the other. In the first place, who is Aaron ? and how would you proceed to strip him ?"

"Aaron ?" repeated Bill thoughtfully; "Aaron ? I never heard of such a person. There's Sharon, you know; but stripping *him* would be out of the question. It's generally all the other way!"

"Sharon's a money-lender, isn't he ?" she asked. "What business have *you* to know anything about him, you wicked young man!"

"Never borrowed a sixpence in my life," protested Bill, which was perfectly true. "But I've been to him often enough lately about this business of Daisy's. We've arranged to get fifteen hundred from *him* alone. Perhaps that is what is meant by stripping him. But it was all to be in hard money; and though I know Sharon sometimes makes you take goods, I

never heard of his sending a fellow bulls or
strong honey, or, indeed, anything but dry sherry
and cigars."

She knit her brows and read the message
again. "I think I have it," said she. '*Strip
Aaron,*'—that must mean ' Stop Sharon.' '*Sell
the Chief,*'—that's ' tell the Colonel.' Then '*fail
immediately*' signifies that the writer means to
cross by the first boat. Where does it come
from—Dublin or Roscommon ? "

" Roscommon," answered Bill. " They're
not much in the habit of telegraphing up there."

" Depend upon it Daisy has dropped into
a good thing. Somebody must have left, or
lent, or *given* him a lot of money. I have it !
I have it ! This is how you must read it,"
she exclaimed, and following the lines with
her taper finger, she put them into sense with
no little exultation, for the benefit of her ad-

miring listener. "'Very strange! Money just arrived. Bills at sight, on Bank of Ireland. Sent by an unknown Friend. Sail immediately. Tell Chief. Consult Agent, and stop Sharon at once. Do not lose a moment.' There, sir, should I, or should I not, make a good expert at the Bank?"

"You're a witch—simply a witch," returned the delighted Bill. "It's regular, downright magic. Of course, that's what he means. Of course, he's come into a fortune. Hurrah! hurrah! Mrs. Lushington, have you any objection? I should like to throw my hat in the street, please, and put my head out of window to shout!"

"I beg you'll put out nothing of the kind!" she answered, laughing. "If you must be a boy, at least be a good boy, and do what I tell you."

"I should think I *would* just!" he protested,

still in his paroxysm of admiration. "You
know more than the examiners at Sandhurst!
You could give *pounds* to the senior department! If you weren't so—I mean if you were
old and ugly—I should really believe what I
said at first, that you're a witch!"

She smiled on him in a very bewitching
manner; but her brains were hard at work the
while recapitulating all she had learned in the
last twenty-four hours, with a pleasant conviction that she had put her puzzle together
at last. Yes, she saw it clearly now. The
registered envelope of which she found the
address, in reverse, on Blanche's blotting-paper
must have contained those very bills mentioned
in Daisy's telegram. It had struck her at the
time that the handwriting was stiff and formal,
as if disguised; but this served to account for
the mysterious announcement of an " unknown

fiend!" She was satisfied that Miss Douglas had sent anonymously the sum he wanted to the man she loved. And that sum Bill had already told her was three thousand pounds—exactly the amount, according to her husband's version, lately borrowed by the General from a notorious money-lender. Was it possible Santanella could thus have stripped one admirer to benefit another? It must be so. Such treachery deserved no mercy, and Mrs. Lushington determined to show none.

She considered how far her visitor might be trusted with this startling discovery. It was as well, she thought, that he should be at least partially enlightened, particularly as the transaction was but little to the credit of any one concerned, and could not, therefore, be made public too soon. So she laid her hand on Bill's coat-sleeve, and observed impressively—

"Never mind about my being old and ugly, but attend to what I say. Daisy, as you call him, has evidently found a good friend. Now, I know who that friend is. Don't ask me how I found it out. I never speak without being sure. That money came from Miss Douglas."

Bill opened his eyes and mouth. "Miss Douglas!" he repeated. "Not the black girl with the black mare!"

"The black girl with the black mare, and no other," she answered. "Miss Douglas has paid his debts, and saved him from ruin. What return can a man make for such generosity as that?"

"She's a trump, and he ought to marry her!" exclaimed the young officer. "No great sacrifice either. Only," he added, on reflection, "she looks a bit of a Tartar—wants her head let quite alone at her fences, I should think. She'd be rather a handful; but Daisy wouldn't mind that.

Yes ; he's bound to marry her, no doubt; and I'll see him through it."

"I quite agree with you," responded Mrs. Lushington, "but I won't have you talk about ladies as if they were hunters. It's bad style, young gentleman, so don't do it again. Now, attend to what I tell you. Jump on that poor horse of yours; it must be very tired of staring into my dining-room windows. Go to your agent, and send *him* to Sharon. Let your Colonel know at once. When Daisy arrives, impress on him all that he is bound in honour to do, and you may come and see me again, whenever you like, to report progress."

So Bill leapt into the saddle in exceedingly good spirits, while Mrs. Lushington sat down to her writing-table, with the self-satisfied sensations of one who has performed an action of provident kindness and good-will.

CHAPTER XXIII.

THE DEBT OF HONOUR.

D AISY'S astonishment, on receiving by
post those documents that restored him
to the world from his vegetation in Roscommon, was no less unbounded than his joy.
When he opened the registered letter, and
bills for the whole amount of his liabilities
fluttered out, he could scarcely believe his eyes.
Then he puzzled himself to no purpose, in
wild speculations as to the friend who had
thus dropped from the skies at his utmost need.
He had an uncle prosperous enough in worldly

matters, but this uncle hated parting with his money, and was, moreover, abroad, whereas the welcome letter bore a London post-mark. He could think of no other relative nor friend rich enough, even if willing, to assist him in so serious a difficulty. The more he considered his good luck, the more inexplicable it appeared; nor, taking his host into consultation, did that worthy's suggestions tend to elucidate the mystery.

In the first place, recalling many similar instances under his own observation, Denis opined that the money must have been hidden up for his guest, long ago, by his great grandmother, in a stocking, and forgotten! Next, that the Prussian Government, having heard of the mare's performances at Punchestown, had bought her for breeding purposes, at such a sum as they considered her marketable value.

And, lastly (standing the more stoutly by this theory, for the failure of its predecessors), that the whole amount had been subscribed under a general vote of the Kildare Street Club, in testimony of their admiration for Daisy's bold riding and straightforward conduct as a sportsman!

Leaving him perfectly satisfied with this explanation, Daisy bid his host an affectionate farewell, and started without delay for London, previously telegraphing to his comrade at Kensington certain information and instructions for his guidance. Warped in its transmission by an imaginative clerk in a hurry, we have seen how this message confused and distracted the honest perceptions of its recipient.

That young officer was sitting down to breakfast, with Venus under his chair, while Benjamin, the badger, poked a cautious nose out of his stronghold in the wardrobe, when the hasty retreat of one animal, and formidable growlings of the other, announced a strange step on the stairs. Immediately Daisy rushed into the room, vociferated for Barney to look after his "traps" and pay the cab, seized a hot plate, wagged his head at his host, and began breakfast without further ceremony.

"Seem peckish, young man," observed Bill, contemplating his friend with extreme satisfaction. "Sick as a fool last night, no doubt, and sharp-set this morning in consequence. Go in for a cutlet, my boy. Another kidney, then. That's right. Have a suck of the lemon, and at him again!"

Munching steadily, Daisy repudiated the imputation of sea-sickness, with the scorn of a practised mariner. "It seems to me that I live on that Channel," said he, "like a ship's-

steward, Bill, or a horse-marine! Well, I've
done with it now, I hope, for some time. How
jolly it is to feel straight again! It's like your
horse getting up, when he's been on his head,
without giving you the crowner you deserve.
It was touch-and-go this time, old chap. I say,
you got my telegram?"

Bill laughed. "I did, indeed!" he answered;
"and a nice mull they made. Read it for yourself."

Thus speaking, he tossed across the break-
fast-table that singular communication which
his unassisted ingenuity had so failed to com-
prehend.

Daisy perused it with no little astonishment.
"The fools!" he exclaimed. "Why, Bill, you
m ust have thought I'd gone mad."

"We *did*," replied Bill gravely. "Stark
staring, my boy. We said we always *had*

considered you 'a hatter,' but not so bad as this."

"*We!*" repeated his friend. "What d'ye mean by *we?* You didn't go jawing about it in the regiment, Bill?"

"When I say we," answered the other, with something of a blush, "I mean me and Mrs. Lushington."

"What had *she* to do with it?" asked Daisy, pushing his plate away, and lighting a cigar. "*She* didn't send the stuff, I'll take my oath!"

"But she knows who did," said Bill, filling a meerschaum pipe of liberal dimensions, with profound gravity.

Then they smoked in silence for several minutes.

"It's a very rum go," observed Daisy, after a prolonged and thoughtful puff. "I don't know when I've been so completely at fault

Tell me what you've heard, Bill, for you *have* heard something, I'm sure. In the first place, how came you to take counsel with Mrs. Lushington?"

"Because she is up to every move in the game," was the answer. "Because she's the cleverest woman in London, and the nicest. Because I was regularly beat, and could think of nobody else to help me at short notice. The telegram said, 'Do not lose a moment.'"

"And what did *she* make of it?" asked Daisy.

"Tumbled to the whole plant in three minutes," answered Bill. "Put the telegram straight—bulls, honey, and all—as easy as wheeling into line. I tell you, we know as much as you do now, and *more*. You've got three 'thou,' Daisy, ready-money down, to do what you like with. Isn't that right?"

Daisy nodded assent.

"The Chief's delighted, and I've sent the agent to Sharon. Luckily, the little beggar's not so unreasonable as we thought he'd be. That reckons up the telegram, doesn't it?"

Again Daisy nodded, smoking serenely.

"Then there's nothing more for you to bother about," continued his host; "and I'm glad of it. Only, next time, Daisy, you won't pull for an old woman, I fancy, in a winning race."

"Nor a young one either," said his friend. "But you haven't told me now who the money came from."

"Can't you guess? Have you no idea?"

"Not the faintest."

"What should you say to Miss Douglas?"

"Miss Douglas!"

By the tone in which Daisy repeated her name, that young lady was obviously the last

person in the world from whom he expected
to receive pecuniary assistance.

Though no longer peaceful, his meditations
seemed deeper than ever. At length he threw
away the end of his cigar with a gesture of
impatience and vexation.

"This is a very disagreeable business," said
he. "Hang it, Bill, I almost wish the money
had never come. I can't send it back, for a
thousand's gone already to our kind old major,
who promised to settle my book at Tattersall's.
I wonder where she got such a sum. By Jove,
it's the handsomest thing I ever heard of!
What would you do, Bill, if you were in my
place ? "

"Do," repeated his friend; "I've no doubt
what I should do. I should order Catamount
round at once ; then I think I'd have a brandy-
and-soda; in ten minutes I'd be at Miss

Douglas's door, and in fifteen I'd have—what d'ye call it ?—proposed to her. Proposed to her, my boy, all according to regulation. I'm not sure how you set about these things. I fancy you go down on your knees; I know you ought to put your arm round their waists ; but lots of fellows could coach you for all that part, and even if you did anything that's not in the book, this is a case of emergency, and, in my opinion, you might chance it ! "

Having thus delivered himself, the speaker assumed a judicial air, smoking severely.

"In plain English, a woman buys one for three thousand pounds!" said Daisy, laughing rather bitterly. "*And only three thousand bid for him. Going ! Going ! ! "*

" *Gone ! ! !* " added Bill, bringing his fist down on the table with a bang that startled the badger, and elicited an angry bark from Venus.

"A deuced good price, too! I only hope I shall fetch half as much when I'm brought to the hammer. Why you ought to be delighted, my good fellow. She's as handsome as paint, and the best horsewoman that ever wore a habit!"

"I don't deny her riding, nor her beauty, nor her merit in every way," said Daisy, somewhat ruefully. "In fact, she's much too good for a fellow like me. But do you mean seriously, Bill, that I must marry her because she has paid my debts?"

"I do, indeed," answered his friend; "and Mrs. Lushington thinks so too."

Before Daisy's eyes rose the vision of an Irish river glancing in the sunshine, with banks of tender green and ripples of molten gold, and a fishing-rod lying neglected on its margin, while a fair, fond face looked loving and trustful in his own.

There are certain hopes akin to the child's soap-bubble which we cherish insensibly, admiring their airy grace and radiant colouring, almost persuading ourselves of their reality, till we apply to them some practical test—then behold! at a touch, the bubble bursts, the dream vanishes, to leave us only a vague sense of injustice, an uncomfortable consciousness of disappointment and disgust.

"I conclude Mrs. Lushington understands these things, and knows exactly what a fellow ought to do," said Daisy, after another pause that denoted he was in no indiscreet hurry to act on that lady's decision.

"Of course she does!" answered Bill. "She's a regular authority, you know, or I wouldn't have gone to her. You couldn't be in safer hands."

Both young men seemed to look on the whole

transaction in the light of a duel, or some such affair of honour, requiring caution no less than courage, and in the conduct of which the opinion of a celebrated practitioner like Mrs. Lushington was invaluable and unimpeachable.

"But, if I—if I don't like her well enough," said poor Daisy, looking very uncomfortable. "Hang it, Bill, when one marries a woman, you know, one's obliged to be always with her. Early breakfast, home to luncheon, family dinner, smoke out of doors, and in by ten o'clock. I shouldn't like it at all; and then perhaps she'd take me to morning visits and croquet parties. Think of that, Bill! Like poor Martingale, whose only holiday is when he gets the belt on, and can't stir out of barracks for four-and-twenty hours. To be sure, Miss Douglas is a good many cuts above Mrs. Martingale ! "

"To be sure she is!" echoed his adviser. "And I dare say, after all, Daisy, it is not quite so bad as we think. Wet days and that you'd have to yourself, you know, and she wouldn't want you when she had a headache. Mrs. Martingale often has headaches, and so should I if I liquored up as freely!"

"But supposing," argued Daisy, "I say only *supposing*, Bill, one liked another girl better; oughtn't that to make a difference?"

"I'm afraid *not*," replied Bill, shaking his head. "I didn't think of putting the case in that way to Mrs. Lushington, but I don't imagine she'd admit the objection. No, no, my boy, it's no use being shifty about it. You've got to jump, and the longer you look, the less you'll like it! If it was a mere matter of business, I wouldn't say a word, but see how the case stands. There are no receipts, no vouchers; she has kept everything dark, that you might feel under no obligation. Hang it, old fellow, it's a regular debt of honour; and there's no way of paying up, that I can see, but this."

Such an argument was felt to be unanswerable.

"A debt of honour," repeated Daisy. "I suppose it is. Very well; I'll set about it at once. I can't begin to-day though."

"Why not?" asked his friend.

"No time," answered the other, who, in many respects, was a true Englishman. "I've got lots of things to do. In the first place, I must have my hair cut, of course."

CHAPTER XXIV.

A LETTER, without date or signature, written in an upright, clerkly hand, correctly spelt, sufficiently well-expressed, and stamped at the General Post Office! St. Josephs had no clue to his correspondent, and could but read the following production over and over again with feelings of irritation and annoyance that increased at each perusal :—

"You have been ill-treated and deceived. A sense of justice compels the writer of these lines to warn you before it is too late.

You are the victim of a conspiracy to plunder and defraud. One cannot bear to see a man of honour robbed by the grossest foul play. General St. Josephs is not asked to believe a bare and unsupported statement. Let him recapitulate certain facts, and judge for himself. He best knows whether he did not lately borrow a large sum of money. He can easily discover if that amount corresponds, to a fraction, with the losses of a young officer celebrated for his horsemanship. Let him ascertain why that person's debts have stood over till now; also, how and when they have been settled. Will he have courage to ask himself, or *somebody* he trusts as himself, whence came these funds that have placed his rival in a position to return to England? Will he weigh the answer in the balance of common-sense; or is he so infatuated by a certain dark lady that he can be fooled with his eyes open, in full light of day? There is no time to lose, or this caution would never have been given. If neglected, the General will regret his incredulity as long as he lives. Most women would appreciate his admiration; many would be more than proud of his regard. There is but one, perhaps, in the world who could thus repay it by injury and deceit. He is entreated to act at once on this communication, and to believe that of all his well-wishers it comes from the sincerest and the most reliable."

Everybody affects to despise anonymous letters. No doubt it is a wise maxim that such communications should be put in the fire at once, and ignored as if they did not exist. Nevertheless, on the majority of mankind they inflict unreasonable anxiety and distress. The sting rankles, though the insect be infinitesimal and contemptible; the blow falls none the less severely that it has been delivered in the dark.

On a nature like the General's such an epistle as the above was calculated to produce the utmost amount of impatience and discomfort. To use a familiar expression, it *worried* him beyond measure. Straightforward in all his dealings, he felt utterly at a loss when he came in contact with mystery or deceit. Nothing could furnish plainer proof of the General's sincere attachment to Miss Douglas than the fortitude with which he confronted certain petty vexations and annoyances inseparable from the love affairs of young and old.

> "Ah me! what perils do environ,
> The man who meddles with cold iron,"

quoth Hudibras; but surely his risk is yet greater, who elects to heat the metal from hilt to point, in the furnace of his own affections, and burns his fingers every time he draws the sword, even in self-defence. To St. Josephs who, after a manhood of hardship, excitement, and some military renown, had arrived at a time of life when comfort and repose are more appreciated, and more desirable every day, nothing could have been so distasteful as the character he now chose to enact, but for her charms, who had cast the part for him, and with whom, by dint of perseverance and fidelity, he hoped to play out the play.

Though he often sighed to remember how heavily he was weighted with his extra burden of years, he never dreamed of retiring from the contest, nor relaxed for one moment in his efforts to attain the goal.

Twenty times was he on the point of destroying a letter that so annoyed him, and twenty times he checked himself, with the reflection, that even this treacherous weapon might be wrested from the enemy, and turned to his own advantage by sincerity and truth. After much cogitation, he ordered his horse, dressed himself carefully, and rode to Miss Douglas's door.

That lady was at home. Luncheon, coming out of the dining-room untouched, met him as he crossed the hall, and the tones of her piano-forte rang in his years, while he went up-stairs. When the door opened she rose from the instrument and turned to greet him with a pale face, showing traces of recent tears.

All his self-command vanished at these tokens of her distress.

"You've been crying, my darling," said he, and taking her hand in both his own, he pressed it fondly to his lips.

It was not a bad beginning. Hitherto he had

always been so formal, so respectful, so unlike a lover; now, when he saw that she was unhappy, the man's real nature broke out, and she liked him none the worse.

Withdrawing her hand, but looking very kindly, and speaking in a softer tone than usual, she bade him take no notice of her agitation.

"I'm nervous," said she. "I often am. You men can't understand these things, but it's better than being cross, at any rate."

"Cross!" he repeated. "Be as cross and as nervous as you like, only make *me* the prop when you require support, and the scapegoat when you want to scold."

"You're too good," said she, her dark eyes filling again, whereat he placed himself very close and took her hand once more. "Far too good for *me!* I've told you so a hundred times. General, shall I confess why

I was—was making such a fool of myself, and what I was thinking of when you came in?"

"If it's painful to *you*, I'd rather not hear it," was his answer. "I want to be associated with the sunshine of your life, Blanche, not its shade."

She shook her head.

"Whoever takes part in *my* life," she replied, "must remain a good deal in the dark. That's what I was coming to. General, it is time you and I should understand each other. I feel I could tell *you* things I would not breathe to any other living being. You're so safe, so honourable, so punctiliously, so *ridiculously* honourable,—and I *like* you for it."

He looked grateful.

"I want you to like me," said he, "better and better every day. I'll try to deserve it."

"They say time works wonders," she answered wistfully, "and I feel I shall;—I *know* I shall. But there are some things I *must* tell you now, while I have the courage. Mind, I am prepared to take all consequences. I have deceived you, General. Deceived you in a way you could never imagine nor forgive."

"So people seem to think," he observed coolly, producing, at the same time, the anonymous letter from his pocket. "I should not have troubled you with such trash, but as you have chosen to make me your father-confessor —perhaps I ought to say your *grand*-father-confessor—this morning, you may as well look through it, before we put that precious production in the fire."

He walked to the window, so as not to see her face while she read it, nor was this little act of delicacy and forbearance lost on such a woman as Blanche Douglas.

Her temper, nevertheless, became thoroughly roused before she got to the end of the letter, causing her to place herself once more in the position of an adversary. Her eyes shone, her brows lowered, and her words came in the tight, concentrated accents of bitter anger, while she bade him turn round, and look her in the face.

"This has only anticipated me," said she, pale and quivering. "I stand here arraigned like any prisoner in the dock, but with no excuses to offer, no defence to make. It is a fine position, truly; but having been fool enough to accept it, I do not mean to shrink from its disgrace. Ask me what questions you will, I am not afraid to answer them."

"Honestly?" said he, "without quibbles or afterthought, and once for all?"

She looked very stern and haughty.

"I am not in the habit of shuffling," she

replied. "I never yet feared results from word or action of mine; and what I say, you may depend upon it I mean."

On the General's face came an expression of confidence and resolution she had never noticed before. Meeting his regard firmly, it occurred to her that so he must have looked when he rode through that Sepoy column, and charged those Russian guns. He was a gallant fellow, no doubt, bold and kind-hearted too.

If he had only been twenty years younger, or even ten !

He spoke rather lower than usual; but every syllable rang clear and true, while his eyes looked frankly and fearlessly into her own.

" Then answer my question once for all. Blanche, will you be my wife ? Without further hesitation or delay ?"

" Let me explain first."

"I ask for no explanation, and will listen to none. Suppose me to repose implicit confidence in the vague accusations of an anonymous slander ;—suppose me to believe you false and fickle, a shameless coquette, and myself an infatuated old fool ; — suppose anything and everything you please ; but first answer the question I ask you from the bottom of my heart, with this anonymous statement—false or true, I care not a jot which—in my hand."

He held it as if about to tear it across and fling it in the grate. She laid a gentle touch on his arm and whispered softly—

"Don't destroy it till I've answered your question.—Yes! There is nobody like you in the world!"

We need not stop to repeat a proverb touching the irreverent persistency of Folly in travelling hand-in-hand with Age. Of what extravagances the General might have been guilty, in his exceeding joy, it is impossible to guess, had she not stopped him at the outset.

" Sit down there," she said, pointing to a corner of the sofa, while establishing herself in an arm-chair on the other side of the fire-place. " Now that you have had your say, perhaps you will let me have *mine!* Hush ! I know what you mean. I take all that for granted. Stay where you are, hold your tongue, and listen to me."

"The first duty of a soldier is obedience," he answered in great glee. " I'll be as steady as I can."

" It is my *right* now to explain," she continued gravely. " Believe me. I most fully appreciate, I never can forget—whatever happened I never *could* forget—the confidence you have shown in me to-day. Depend upon it, when you trust people so unreservedly, you make it *impossible* for them to deceive. I have always honoured and admired you. During the last hour I have learned to—to—well—to think you deserve more than honour and esteem. Any woman might be proud and happy — yes — happy to belong to you. But now, if I am to be your wife—don't interrupt. Well, *as* I am to be your wife, you must let we tell you everything —everything—or I recall my promise."

"Don't do that," he answered playfully. "But mind, I'm quite satisfied with you as you are, and ask to know *nothing.*"

She hesitated, and the colour came to her brow while she completed her confession. "You—you lent me some money, you know; *gave* it me, I ought to say, for I'm quite sure you never expected to see it back again. It was a good deal. Don't contradict. It *was* a good deal, and I wonder how I could have the face to ask for it. But I didn't want it for myself. It was to save from utter ruin a very old and dear friend."

"I know all about it," said he cheerfully. "At least, I can guess. Very glad it should be so well employed. But all that was *your* business, not mine."

"And you never even asked who got it!" she continued, while again there gathered a mist to veil her large dark eyes.

"My dear Blanche," he answered, "I was only too happy to be of service to you. Surely it was your own, to employ as you liked. I don't want to know any more about it, even now."

"But you *must* know," she urged. "I've been going to tell you ever so often, but something always interrupted us; and once, when

I had almost got it out, the words seemed to
die away on my lips. Listen. You know I'm
not very young."

He bowed in silence. The reflection naturally
presented itself that if *she* were not very young,
he must be very old.

Miss Douglas proceeded, with her eyes fixed
on her listener, as if she was looking at something a long way off.

"Of course I've seen and known lots of
people in my life, and had some great friends—
I mean *real* friends—that I would have made
any sacrifice to serve. Amongst these was
Mr. Walters. I used to call him Daisy.
General, I—I liked him better than all the
rest. Better than anybody in the world——"

"And now?" asked the General anxiously,
but carrying a bold front notwithstanding.

"*Now*, I know I was mistaken," she replied.

"Though that's not the question. Well, after that horrid race—when my beautiful mare ought to have won, and *didn't*—I knew Daisy—Mr. Walters, I mean—had lost more than he could afford to pay—in plain English, he was ruined; and worse, wouldn't be able to show, unless somebody came to the rescue. I hadn't got the money myself. Not a hundredth part of it! So I asked *you*, and—and—sent it all to *him*. Now you know the whole business."

"I knew it long ago," said he gently. "At least, I might have known it, had I ever allowed the subject to enter my head. Does *he* know it too, do you think, Blanche?"

"Good heavens! No!" she exclaimed. "That *would* be a complication. You don't think there's a chance of it! I took every care—every precaution. What *should* I do? General, what would you advise?"

He smiled to mark how she was beginning to depend on him, drawing a good augury from this alteration in her character, and would no doubt have replied in exceedingly affectionate terms, but that he was interrupted by the opening of the drawing-room door, and entrance of a servant, who, in a matter-of-fact voice, announced a visitor—

"Mr. Walters!"

Blanche turned white to her lips, and muttered rapidly, "Won't you stay, General? *Do!*"

But the General had already possessed himself of his hat, and, with an air of good-humoured confidence, that she felt did honour both to herself and him, took a courteous leave of his hostess, and gave a hearty greeting to the new-comer as they passed each other on the threshold.

"I think I've won the battle," muttered the old soldier, mounting his horse briskly in the street; "though I've left the enemy in possession of the ground!"

CHAPTER XXV.

A SATISFACTORY ANSWER.

D AISY, with his hair cut exceedingly short, as denoting that he was on the eve of some great crisis in life, entered the apartment in the sheepish manner of a visitor who is not quite sure about his reception. Though usually of cheerful and confident bearing, denoting no want of a certain self-assertion, which the present generation call "cheek," all his audacity seemed to have deserted him, and he planted himself in the centre of the carpet, with his hat in his hand, like the poor, spiritless bridegroom at Netherby, who stood "dangling his bonnet and plume" while his affianced and her bridesmaids were making eyes at young Lochinvar.

Miss Douglas, too, required a breathing-space to restore her self-command. When they had shaken hands, it was at least a minute before either could find anything to say.

The absurdity of the situation struck them both, but the lady was the first to recover her presence of mind; and, with a laugh not the least genuine, welcomed him back to England, demanding the latest news from Paddy-land.

"You've been at Cormac's-town, of course," said she. "You can tell us all about dear Lady Mary, and your pretty friend Norah. I hope she asked to be remembered to *me.*"

He blushed up to his eyes, turning his hat in his hands, as if he would fain creep into it bodily, and hide himself from notice in the crown.

She saw her advantage, and gained courage every minute, so as to stifle and keep down the gnawing pain that made her so sick at heart.

"I wonder Norah trusts you in London," she continued, with another of those forced smiles. "I suppose you're only on short leave, as you call it, and mean to go back directly. Will you have the black mare to ride, while you are in town? I've taken great care of her, and she's looking beautiful!"

To her own ear, if not to his, there was a catch in her breath while she spoke the last words, that warned her she would need all her self-command before the play was played out.

He thanked her kindly enough, while he declined the offer; but his tone was so grave, so sorrowful, that she could keep up the affectation of levity no longer.

"What is it?" she asked, in an altered voice. "Daisy!—Mr. Walters! What is the matter? Are you offended? I was only joking about Norah."

"Offended!" he repeated. "How could I ever be offended with *you*? But I didn't come here to talk about Miss Macormac, nor even Satanella, except in so far as the mare is connected with your generosity and kindness."

"What do you mean?" she asked, in considerable trepidation. "*You* were the generous one, for you gave me the best hunter in your stable, without being asked."

"As if you had not bought her over and over again!" he exclaimed, finding voice and words and courage now that he was approaching the important topic. "Miss Douglas, it's no use

denying your good deeds, nor pretending to
ignore their magnificence. It was only yesterday I learned the real name of my *unknown
friend !* I tell you, that money of yours saved
me from utter ruin—worse than ruin, from such
disgrace as if I had committed a felony, and
been sent to prison ! "

" I'm sure you look as if you had just come
out of one," she interposed, "with that cropped
head. Why do you let them cut your hair
so short ? It makes you hideous ! "

" Never mind my cropped head," he continued, somewhat baffled by the interruption.
" I hurried here at once, to thank you with all
my heart, as the best friend I ever had in the
world."

" Well, you've done it," said she. " That's
quite enough. Now let us talk of something
else."

" But I *haven't* done it," protested Daisy, gathering, from the obstacles in his way, a certain inclination to his task or at least a determination to go through with it. " I haven't said half what I've got to say, nor a quarter of what I feel. You have shown that you consider me a near and dear friend. You have given me the plainest possible proof of your confidence and esteem. All this instigates me—or rather induces me, or, shall I say, encourages me—to hope, or perhaps persuade myself of some probability. In short, Miss Douglas—can't you help a fellow out with what he's got to say ? "

Floundering about in search of the right expressions, she would have liked him to go on for an hour. It was delightful to be even on the brink of that paradise from which she must presently exclude herself for ever with her own hands, and she forbore to interrupt him till he came to a dead stop for want of words.

"Nonsense!" she said. "Any friend would have done as much who had the power. It's nothing to make a fuss about. I'm glad you're out of the scrape, and there's an end of it."

"You were always generous," he exclaimed. "You ought to have been a man; I've said so a hundred times—only it's lucky you're *not*, or I couldn't ask you a question that I don't know how to put in the right form."

She turned pale as death. It was come, then, at last—that moment to which she had once looked forward as a glimpse of happiness too exquisite for mortal senses. Here was the enchanted cup pressed to her very lip, and she must not taste it—must withdraw her very eyes from the insidious drink. And yet even now she felt a certain sense of disappointment in her triumph, a vague misgiving that the proffered draught was flatter than it should be, as if the bottle had been already opened to slake another's thirst.

" Better not ask," she said, " if the words don't come naturally,—if the answer is sure to be *no*."

In his intense relief he never marked the piteous tone of her voice, nor the tremble of agony passing over her face, like the flicker of a fire on a marble bust, to leave its features more fixed and rigid than before.

Even in her keen suffering she wished to spare *him*. Already she was beginning to long for the dull insensibility that must succeed this hour of mental conflict, as bodily numbness is the merciful result of pain. She dreaded the possibility that his disappointment should be anything like her own, and would fain have modified the blow she had no choice but to inflict.

Daisy, however, with good reasons no doubt, was resolved to rush on his fate the more obstinately, as it seemed, because of the endeavours to spare both him and herself.

"I am a plain-spoken fellow," said he, "and —and—tolerably straightforward, as times go. I'm not much used to this kind of thing—at least, I've never regularly asked such a question before. You mustn't be offended, Miss Douglas, if I don't go the right way to work. But—but —it seems so odd that you should have come in and paid my debts for me ! Don't you think I ought—or don't you think *you* ought—in short, I've come here on purpose to ask you to marry me. I'm not half good enough, I know, and lots of fellows would make you better husbands, I'm afraid. But, really now—without joking—won't you try?"

He had got into the spirit of the thing, and went on more swimmingly than he could have hoped. There was almost a ring of truth in his appeal, for Daisy's was a temperament that flung itself keenly into the excitement of the moment, gathering ardour from the very sense of pursuit. As he said of himself, "He never could help riding, if he got a start!"   ·

And Miss Douglas shook in every limb while she listened with a wan, weary face and white lips, parted in a rigid smile. It was not that she was unaccustomed to solicitations of a like nature; whatever might be her previous ex-perience, scarcely an hour had passed since she sustained a similar attack—and surely to accept an offer of marriage ought to be more

subversive of the nervous system than to refuse;
yet she could hardly have betrayed deeper emo-
tion had she been trembling in the balance
between life and death.

That was a brave heart of hers, or it must
have failed to keep its own rebellion down so
firmly, and gather strength to answer in a calm,
collected voice—

"There are some things it is better not to
think about, for they can never be, and this is
one of them."

How little she knew what was passing in his
mind! How little she suspected that *her* sentence was *his* reprieve! And yet his self-love
was galled. He had made a narrow escape,
and was thankful, no doubt, but felt somewhat
disappointed, too, that his danger had not been
greater still.

"Do you mean it?" said he. "Well, you'll

forgive my presumption, and—and—you won't forget I asked you."

" *Forget !* ——"

It was all she said; but a man must have been both blind and deaf not to have marked the tone in which those syllables were uttered, the look that accompanied them. Daisy brandished his hat, thinking it high time to go, lest his sentence should be commuted, and his doom revoked.

, She put her hand to her throat, as if she must choke; but mastered her feelings with an effort, forcing herself to speak calmly and distinctly now, on a subject that must never be approached again.

"Do not think I undervalue your offer," she said, gathering fortitude with every word; " do not think me hard, or changeable, or unfeeling. If you must not make me happy, at least you have made me very proud; and if everything had turned out differently, I do hope I might have proved worthy to be your wife. You're not angry with me, are you? And you won't hate me because it's impossible?"

"Not the least!" exclaimed Daisy eagerly. "Don't think it for a moment! Please not to make yourself unhappy about *me*."

"I *am* worthy to be your friend," she continued, saddened, and it may be a little vexed by this remarkable exhibition of self-denial; "and *as* a friend I feel I owe you some explanation, beyond a bare 'No, I won't.' It ought rather to be 'No, I *can't;*' because— because, to tell you the honest truth, I have promised somebody else!"

"I wish you joy, with all my heart!" he exclaimed gaily, and not the least like an unsuccessful suitor. "I hope you'll be as happy as the day is long! When is it to be? You'll send me an invitation to the wedding, won't you?"

Her heart was very sore. He did not even ask the name of his fortunate rival, and he could hardly have looked more pleased, she thought, if he had been going to marry her himself.

" I don't know about that," she answered, shaking her head sadly. " At any rate, I shall not see you again for a long time. Good-bye, Daisy," and she held out a cold hand that trembled very much.

" Good-bye," said he, pressing it cordially. " I shall never forget your kindness. Good-bye."

Then the door shut, and he was gone.

Blanche Douglas sank into a sofa, and sat there looking at the opposite wall, without moving hand or foot, till the long summer's

day waned into darkness and her servant came
with lights. She neither wept, nor moaned,
nor muttered broken sentences, but remained
perfectly motionless, like a statue, and in all
those hours she asked herself but one question—
"Do I love this man ? and, if so, how can I
ever bear to marry the other?"

CHAPTER XXVI.

AFTERNOON TEA.

"I WISH you'd come, Daisy. You've no idea what it is, facing all those swells by oneself!"

"I have *not* the cheek," was Daisy's reply. "They would chaff one so awfully, if they knew. No, Bill, I'll see you through anything but that."

"Then I must show the best front I can without a support," said the other ruefully. "Why can't she let me off these tea-fights? They're cruelly slow. I don't see the good of them."

"*She* does," replied Daisy. "Not a woman

in London knows what she is about better than
Mrs. Lushington.

"How d'ye mean?" asked his less worldly-
minded friend.

"Why, you see," explained Daisy, "one
great advantage of living in this wicked town
is, that you've no duty towards your neighbour. People don't care two straws what you
do, or how you do it, so long as you keep your
own line without crossing theirs. They'll give
you the best of everything, and ask for no
return, if only you'll pretend to be glad to see
them when you meet, and not forget them when
you go away. That's the secret of morning-
visits, card-leaving, wedding-presents, and the
whole of the sham. Now Mrs. Lushington goes
everywhere, and never has a ball, nor a drum,
nor even a large dinner-party of her own, but
she says to her friends, 'I love you dearly, I

can't exist without you. Come and see me every Wednesday, except the Derby day, all the London season through, from five to seven p.m. I'll swear to be at home, and I'll give you a cup of tea!' So, for nine-pen'orth of milk, and some hot water, she repays the hospitalities of a nation. She's pleased, the world is gratified, and nobody's bored but *you*. It's all humbug, that's the truth, and I'm very glad I'm so soon to be out of it!"

"But you won't leave the regiment?" said his brother officer kindly.

"Not if I know it!" was the hearty response. "Norah likes soldiering, and old Macormac doesn't care what we do, if we only visit *him* in the hunting season. Besides, my uncle put that in the conditions when he 'parted,' which he did freely enough, I am bound to admit, considering all things."

"You've not been long about it," observed Soldier Bill in a tone of admiration. "It's little more than a month since you pulled through after that 'facer' at Punchestown; and now, here you are, booked to one lady, after proposing to another, provided with settlements, *trousseau*, bridesmaids, and very likely a bishop to marry you. Hang it, Daisy, I've got an uncle *smothered* in lawn; I'll give him the straight tip, and ask him to tie you up fast."

"You'll have to leave the Park at once," was Daisy's reply, "or you'll be returned absent when the parade is formed. You know, Bill, you *daren't* be late, for your life."

The two young men were by this time at Albert Gate, having spent a pleasant half-hour together on a couple of penny chairs, while the strange medley passed before them that throngs Hyde Park on every summer's afternoon. Daisy

was far happier than he either hoped or de
served. After Satanella's refusal, he had felt
at liberty to follow the dictates of his own
heart, and lost no time in prosecuting his suit
with Norah Macormac. The objections that
might have arisen from want of means were
anticipated by his uncle's unlooked for liberality, and he was to be married as soon as the
necessary arrangements could be made, though,
in consideration of his late doings, the engage-
ment was at present to be kept a profound
secret.

Notwithstanding some worldly wisdom, Daisy
could believe that such secrets divided amongst
half-a-dozen people would not become the
property of half-a-hundred.

In a mood like his, a man requires no companion but his own thoughts. We will rather
accompany Soldier Bill, as he picks his way

into Belgravia, stepping daintily over the
muddy crossings, cursing the water-carts, and
trying to preserve the polish of his boots, up to
Mrs. Lushington's door.

Yet into those shining boots his heart seemed
almost sinking, when he marked a long line of
carriages in the streets, a crowd of footmen on
the steps and pavement. No man alive had
better nerve than Bill, to ride, or fight, or swim,
or face any physical danger; but his hands
turned cold, and his face hot, when about to
confront strange ladies, either singly or in
masses; and for him, the rustling of muslin was
as the shaking of a standard to the inex-
perienced charger, a signal of unknown danger,
a flutter of terror and dismay.

Nevertheless, he mastered his weakness, following his own name resolutely up-stairs, in a
white heat no doubt, yet supported by the

calmness of despair. Fortunately, he found his hostess at her drawing-room door. The favourable greeting she accorded him would have re-assured the most diffident of men.

"You're a good boy," she whispered, with a squeeze of his hand. "I was almost afraid you wouldn't come. Stay near the door, while I do the civil to the arch-duchess. I'll be back directly. I've got something very particular to ask you."

So, while Mrs. Lushington did homage (in French, to the arch-duchess, who was old, fat, good-humoured, and very sleepy, Bill took up a position from which he could pass the inmates of the apartment in review. Observing his welcome by their hostess, and knowing *who he was*, two or three magnificent ladies thought it not derogatory to afford him a gracious bow; and as they forbore to engage him in discourse,

—a visitation of which Bill had fearful misgivings,—he soon felt sufficiently at ease to
inspect unconcernedly, and in detail, the several
individuals who constituted the crush.

It was a regular London gathering, in the
full-tide of the season, consisting of the best-
dressed, best-looking, and idlest people in town.
There seemed an excess of ladies, as usual; but
who would complain of a summer market, that
it was over stocked with flowers? While of the
uglier sex, the specimens were either very
young or very mature. There was scarcely a
man to be seen between thirty and forty, but a
glut of young gentlemen, some too much and
some too little at their ease, with a liberal
sprinkling of ancient dandies, irreproachable in
manners, and worthier members of society, we
may be permitted to hope, than society believed. A few notabilities were thrown in, of

course : the arch-duchess aforesaid ; a missionary, who had been tortured by the Chinese, dark, sallow, and of a physiognomy that went far to extenuate the cruelty of the Celestials ; a lady who had spent two years at Thebes, and, perhaps for that reason, dressed almost as low as the Egyptian Sphinx ; a statesman out of office ; a celebrated preacher at issue with his bishop ; a foreign minister ; a London banker ; and a man everybody knew, who wrote books nobody read. Besides these, there was the usual complement of ladies who gave, and ladies who went to, balls ; married women addicted to flirting ; single ladies not averse to it ; stout mammas in gorgeous apparel ; tall girls with baby-faces promising future beauty ; a powdered footman winding, like an eel, through the throng ; Frank Lushington himself, looking at his watch to see how soon it would be over ;

and pretty Bessie Gordon, fresh and smiling, superintending the tea.

All this Bill took in, wondering. It seemed such a strange way of spending a bright summer's afternoon, in weather that had come on purpose for cricket, boating, yachting, all sorts of out-of-door pursuits. Putting himself beside the question, for he felt as much on duty as if he had the belt on in a barrack-yard, it puzzled him to discover the spell that brought all these people together, in a hot room, at six o'clock in the day. Was it sheer idleness, or the love of talking, or only the follow-my-leader instinct of pigs and sheep? Catching sight of General St. Josephs and Miss Douglas conversing apart in a corner, he determined that it must be a motive stronger than any of these; and looking down on her broad deep shoulders, marvelled how such motive might affect his next neighbour, a lady of sixty years, weighing some sixteen stone.

It is fair to suppose, therefore, that Bill was as yet himself untouched. His intimacy with Mrs. Lushington, while sharpening his wits and polishing his manners, served, no doubt, to dispel those illusions of romance that all young men are prone to cherish, more or less; and Soldier Bill, with his fresh cheeks and simple heart, believed he was becoming a thorough philosopher, an experienced man of the world, rating human weaknesses at their real value, and walking about the battle of life sheathed in armour of proof. Honest Bill! How little he dreamt that his immunity was only a question of time. The hour had not yet come—nor the woman!

Far different was St. Josephs. If ever man exulted in bondage and seemed proud to rattle his chains, that man was the captive General. He never missed an opportunity of attending his conqueror: riding in the Park—"walking in the Zoo"—waiting about at balls, drums, crush-rooms, and play-houses,—he never left her side.

Miss Douglas, loathing her own ingratitude, was weary of her life. Even Bill could not help remarking the pale cheeks, the heavy eyes, the dull lassitude of gait and bearing, that denoted the feverish unrest of one who is sick at heart.

He trod on a chaperone's skirt, and omitted to beg pardon; he stumbled against his uncle, the bishop, and forgot to ask after his aunt. So taken up was he with the faded looks of Miss Douglas, that he neither remembered where he was, nor why he came, and only recovered consciousness with the rustle of Mrs. Lushington's dress and her pleasant voice in his ear.

"Give me your arm," said she, pushing on

through her guests, with many winning smiles, "and take me into the little room for some tea."

Though a short distance, it was a long passage. She had something pleasant to say to everybody, as she threaded the crowd; but it could be no difficult task for so experienced a campaigner, on her own ground, to take up any position she required. And Bill found himself established at last by her side, in a corner, where they were neither overlooked nor overheard.

"Now I want to know if it's true?" said she, dashing into the subject at once. " *You* can tell, if anybody can, and I'm sure you have no secrets from *me.*"

"If *what's* true?" asked Bill, gulping tea that made him hotter than ever.

"Don't be stupid!" was her reply. "Why,

about Daisy of course. Is he going to marry that Irish girl ? I want to find out at once."

"Well, it's no use denying it," stammered Bill, somewhat unwillingly. "But it's a dead secret, Mrs. Lushington, and of course it goes no farther."

"Oh, of course!" she repeated. "Don't you know how safe I am ? But you're quite sure of it ? You have it from himself?"

"I've got to be his best man," returned Bill, by no means triumphantly. "You'll coach me up a little, won't you, before the day ? I haven't an idea what to do."

She laughed merrily.

"Make love to the bridesmaids, of course," she answered. "Irish, no doubt, every one of them. I'm not quite sure I shall give you leave."

"I can't get out of it!" exclaimed Bill.

"He's such a 'pal,' you know, and a brother-officer, and all."

She was amused at his simplicity.

"I don't want you to get out of it," she answered still laughing. "I can't tell what sort of a best man you'll make, but you're not half a bad boy. You deserve something for coming to-day. Dine with us to-morrow—nobody but the Gordon girls and a stray man. I must go and see the great lady off. That's the worst of royalty. Good-bye;" and she sailed away, leaving Bill somewhat disconcerted by misgivings that he had been guilty of a breach of trust.

The party was thinning visibly up-stairs, while people transferred themselves with one accord to the hall and staircase, many appearing to consider this the pleasantest part of the entertainment. Mrs. Lushington had scarcely yet found time to speak three words to Blanche

Douglas, but she caught her dear friend now, on the eve of departure, and held her fast. The General had gone to look for his ladye-love's carriage. They were alone in Mr. Lushington's snuggery, converted (though not innocent of tobacco smoke) into a cloak-room for the occasion.

"So good of you to come, dear Blanche, and to bring *him*" (with a meaning smile). "I waited to pounce on you *here*. I've got *such* a piece of news for you!"

Miss Douglas looked as if nothing above, upon, or under the earth could afford her the slightest interest, but she was obliged to profess a polite curiosity.

"Who *do* you think is going to be married? —immediately! next week, I believe. Who but our friend Daisy!"

The shot told. Though Miss Douglas received

it with the self-command of a practised duellist, so keen an observer as her friend did not fail to mark a quiver of the eye-lids, a tightening of the lips, and a grey hue creeping gradually over the face.

" Our fickle friend Daisy, of all people in the world!" continued Mrs. Lushington. " It only shows how we poor women can be deceived. I sometimes fancied he admired *me*, and I never doubted but he cared for *you*, whereas he has gone and fallen a victim to that wild Irish girl of Lady Mary Macormac's—the pretty one— that was such a friend of yours."

" I always thought he admired her," answered Miss Douglas in a very feeble voice. " I ought to write and wish Norah joy. Are you quite sure it's true ? "

" Quite ! " was the reply. " My authority is his own best man."

Fortunately the General appeared at this juncture, with tidings of the carriage, while, through a vista of footmen, might be seen at the open door a brougham-horse on his hind-legs, impatient of delay.

"Good-bye, dear Blanche! You look so tired. I hope you haven't done too much."

"Good-bye, dear Clara! I've had such a pleasant afternoon."

Putting her into the carriage, the General's kind heart melted within him. She looked so pale and worn. She clung so confidingly, so dejectedly to his arm. She pressed his hand so affectionately when he bade her good-bye, and seemed so loth to let it go, that but for the eyes of all England, which every man believes are fixed on himself alone, he would have sprung in, too, and driven off with her then and there.

But he consoled himself with the certainty of

seeing her next day. That comfort accompanied him to his bachelor lodgings, where he dressed, and lasted all through a regimental dinner at the London Tavern.

While a distinguished leader proposed his health, alluding in flattering terms to the services he had rendered and the dangers he had faced, General St. Josephs was thinking far less of his short soldierlike reply than of the pale face and the dark eyes that would so surely greet him on the morrow, of the future about to open before him at last, that would make amends for a life of war and turmoil, with its gentle solace of love and confidence and repose.

CHAPTER XXVII.

A HARD MORSEL.

L IKE the feasts of Apicius, that dinner at the London Tavern was protracted to an unconscionable length.   Its dishes were rich, various, and indigestible, nothing being served *au naturel* and without "garnish" but the brave simplicity of the guests.

"Wines too there were that would have slain young Ammon;"

and old comrades seldom part under such conditions, without the consumption of much tobacco in the small hours.   Nevertheless, St. Josephs

rose next morning fresh and hopeful as a boy.
He ordered his horse for an early canter in the
Park, and shared the Row with divers young
ladies of tender years, but dauntless courage,
who crammed their ponies along at a pace that
caused manes and tails and golden hair to float
horizontal on the breeze, defiant even of that
mounted inspector, whose heart, though pro-
fessionally intolerant of " furious riding," softened to a pigmy with snub nose and rosy
cheeks, on a tiny quadruped, as round, as fat,
and as saucy-looking as itself.

St. Josephs felt in charity with all mankind,
and returned to breakfast so light of heart, that
he ought to have known, under the invariable
law of compensation, some great misfortune was
in store.

He had little appetite ; happiness, like sorrow,
when excessive, never wants to eat ; but he

dressed himself again with the utmost care, and after exhausting every expedient to while away the dragging hours, started at half-past eleven for the abode of his ladye-love.

Do ˻what he would, it was scarcely twelve when he arrived at her door, where his summons remained so long unanswered, that he had leisure to speculate on the possibility of Miss Douglas being indisposed and not yet awake. So he rang next time, stealthily, and, as it were, under protest, but in vain.

The General then applied himself to the area-bell. "They'll come directly now," he argued; "they'll think it's the beer!" And sure enough the street-door was quickly unfastened, with more turning of keys, clanking of chains, and withdrawal of bolts than is usual during the middle of the season, in the middle of the day.

A very grimy old woman met him on the threshold, and peering suspiciously out of her keen, deep-set eyes, demanded his business in a hoarse voice, suggestive of gin.

"Miss Douglas b'aint here," was the startling answer to his inquiries. "She be gone away for good. Hoff this morning, I shouldn't wonder, afore you was out of bed."

"Gone!" he gasped. "This morning! Did she leave no message?"

"None that I knows of. The servants didn't say nothink about it; leastways, not to *me*."

"But she's coming back?"

"Not likely! The maid *did* suppose as they was a-going for good and all. It's no business of mine. I'm not Miss Douglas's servant. I'm a taking care of the 'ouse for the landlord, I am. It's time I was a-tidying of it up now."

With this broad hint, she proceeded to shut

the door in his face, when the General, recovering his presence of mind, made use of the only
argument his experience had taught him was
universal and conclusive.

Her frown relaxed with the touch of money
on her palm. "You're a gentleman, you are,"
she observed approvingly. "Won't ye step in,
sir? It's bad talking with the door in your
'and."

He complied, and sat down on one of the
bare hall-chairs, feeling as he had felt once
before, when badly hit, in the Punjaub.

She went on with her dusting, talking all
the time. "You see they sent round for me
first thing in the morning; and I says to Mrs.
Jones—that's my landlady, sir,"—(dropping a
curtsey),—"'Mrs. Jones,' says I, 'whatever they
can be up to,' says I, 'making such an early
flitting?' says I——"

" But do you mean they've left no letter?"
he interrupted, starting from his seat; "no
directions—no address? Are all the servants
gone? Has Miss Douglas taken much luggage
with her. Did she go away in a cab? Oh,
woman! woman! tell me all you know! It's
a matter of life and death!"

She looked at him askance, privately opining
that, early as it was, the gentleman had been
drinking, and sympathising with him none the
less for that impression.

"They're off," said she stubbornly; "and
they've took everythink along with them—bags
and boxes, and what not. There was a man
round after the keys—not half an hour gone.
I should say as they wasn't coming back, none
of 'em, no more."

This redundancy of negatives forcibly expressed her hopelessness of their return, and

the General's good sense told him it was time
wasted to cross-question his informant any
further. Summoning his energies, he reflected
that the post-office would be the best place
whereat to prosecute inquiries, so he bade the
old woman farewell, with all the fortitude he
could muster, leaving her much impressed by
his manners, bearing, and profuse liberality.

At the post-office, however (an Italian ware-
house round the corner), they knew nothing.
The General, at his wits'-end, bethought him of
those livery-stables where Satanella kept her
namesake, the redoubtable black mare.

Here his plight excited the utmost interest
and commiseration. "Certainly. The General
should have all the assistance in their power.
Of course, the lady had forgotten to leave her
address, no doubt. Ladies *was* careless, sometimes, in such matters. A *beautiful* 'orse-

woman," the livery-stable keeper understood, "an' kep' two remarkably clever ones for her own riding. Had an idea they went away this very morning. Might be mistaken. John could tell. John was the head-ostler. It was John's business to know." So a bell rang, and John, in a long-sleeved waistcoat, sleeking a close-cropped head, appeared forthwith.

"Black mare and chesnut 'oss," said John decidedly. "Gone this morning; groom took with him saddles, clothing, and everything. Paid up to the end of their week. Looked like travelling—had their knee-caps on. Groom a close chap; wouldn't say where. Wish he (John) could find out. Left a setting-muzzle behind, and would like to send it after him."

There seemed nothing to be done here, and the General was fain to retrace his steps, hurt, anxious angry, and more puzzled when he reached home than he had ever been in his life.

For an hour or two, the whole thing seemed so impossible, and the absurdity of the situation struck him as so ridiculous, that he sat idly in his chair to wait for tidings. In this nineteenth century, he told himself, people could not disappear from the surface of society, and leave no sign. Rather, like the sea-bird diving in the waves, if they go down in one place, they must come up in another. There were no kidnappings now, no sendings off to the Plantations, no forcible abductions of ladies, young or old. Then his heart turned sick, and his blood ran cold, while he recalled more than one instance in his own experience, where individuals had suddenly vanished from their homes and never been heard of again.

Stung to action by such thoughts, he collected

his ideas to organise a comprehensive system of pursuit, that should embrace inquiries at all the railway-stations, cab-stands, and turnpikes in and about the metropolis, with the assistance of Scotland Yard in the background. Then he remembered how an old brother-officer had told him, only the other day, of a similar search made by himself, and attended with success. So he resolved to consult that comrade without delay. It was now two o'clock. He would find him eating luncheon at his Club. In five minutes the General was in a Hansom cab, and in less than ten, leaped out on the steps of that military resort.

Had he gone there an hour ago, it would have spared him a good deal of mental agitation, though perhaps any amount of anxiety would have been preferable to the dull, sickening resignation which succeeded a blow that could no longer be modified, parried, nor escaped. In after-times, the General looked back to those ten minutes in the Hansom cab as the close of an era in his life. Henceforth, every object in nature seemed to have lost something of its colouring, and the sun never shone so bright again.

In the hall an obsequious porter handed him a letter. He staggered when he recognised the familiar hand-writing on the envelope, and drew his breath hard for the effort before he tore it open.

There were several pages, some of them crossed. He retired to the strangers' room, and sat down to pursue the death-warrant of his happiness.

"You will forgive me," it began, "because you are the kindest, the best, the most generous of men; but I should never forgive myself the blow I feel I am now inflicting, were it not that I regard your pride, your character, your high sense of honour, before your happiness. General, I am unfit to be your wife : not because my antecedents are somewhat obscure—*you* know my history, and that I have no reason to be ashamed of it; not because I undervalue the happiness of so high and enviable a lot—any woman, as I have told you more than once, would be proud of your choice; but because you deserve, and could so well appreciate, the unalloyed affection, the complete devotion, that are not mine to give. *Your* wife should have no thought but for you, no hopes independent of you, no memories in which you do not form a part. She should be wrapped up in your existence, identified with you, body and soul. All this I am *not.* I never have been—I never *can* be now. Had I entertained a lower opinion of your merits, admired and *cared for* you less, I would have kept my promise faithfully, and we might have jogged on like many another couple, comfortably enough. But *you* ought to win more than mere *comfort* in married life. You merit, and would expect, *happiness.* How could I bear to see my hero disappointed? For you are my hero—my beau-ideal of a gentleman—and my standard is a very high one, or you and I had never been so unhappy as I firmly believe we both are at this moment. It is in vain to regret, and murmur, and speculate on what might have been, if everything, including one's own identity, were different. There is but one line to take now, even at the eleventh hour. Some day you will acknowledge that I was right. We must never meet again. I have taken such precautions as can baffle, I do believe, even your energy and resource. You

have often said nobody was so determined when
I had made up my mind. I am resolved that
you shall never find out what has become of
me; and I entreat you—I adjure you—if you
love me—nay, as you love me—not to try! So
now, farewell—a long farewell, that it pains me
sore to say. I shall never forget you. In all
my conflict of feelings, in all my self-reproach
and bitter sorrow, when I think of your pain,
I cannot bring myself to wish we had never
met. I am proud of your notice and your
regard—proud to remain under obligations to
you—proud to have loved you so far as my
false, wicked nature had the power. Even now
I can say, though you put me out of your heart,
do not let me pass entirely from your memory.
Think sometimes, and not unkindly, of your
wilful, wayward—

"BLANCHE."

So it was all over.

"It's a good letter," murmured the General; "but I prefer the one Julia wrote to Juan." Then he read it through again, and found, as is usually the case, that the second perusal reversed his impression of the first. Did she *really* mean he was to abstain from all attempt to follow her? He examined the envelope; it bore the stamp of the General Post Office; the contents certainly afforded him no clue, yet, judging by analogy, he argued that no woman would lay such stress on the precautions she had taken if she did not wish their efficacy to be proved. When he found, however, that nothing short of police-detectives and news-paper advertisements would avail him, he took a juster view of her intentions, and in the chivalry of his nature resolved that under this great affliction, as in every other condition of their acquaintance, he would yield implicitly to her wish.

So he went back into the world, grave, kindly, and courteous as before. There were a few more gray hairs in his whiskers, and he avoided ladies' society altogether; otherwise, to the unobservant eye, he was little altered; but a dear old friend whom he had nursed through cholera at Varna, and dragged from under a dead horse at Lucknow, took him into a bay-window of the club-library, and thus addressed him—

"My good fellow, you're looking shamefully seedy. Idleness never suited you. Nothing like work to keep old horses sound. Why don't you apply for employment? There's always something to do in the East."

CHAPTER XXVIII.

"SEEKING REST AND FINDING NONE."

BUT great nations do not plunge recklessly into war, nor even do mountain tribes rise suddenly in rebellion because an elderly gentleman is suffering like some sentimental school-girl from a disappointment of the heart. General St. Josephs extorted, indeed, from a great personage the promise that if anything turned up he would not be forgotten, and was fain to content himself, for the time, with a pledge in which he knew he could place implicit trust. So the weary, hot months dragged on,

and he remained in London, solitary, silent,
pre-occupied, wandering about the scenes of
his former happiness, like a ghost. He went
yachting, indeed, with one friend, and agreed
on a pedestrian excursion through Switzerland
with another; but the " sad sea waves " were
too sad for him to endure, and the energy that
should have taken him over a mountain, or up
a glacier, seemed to fail with the purchase of
a knapsack and the perusal of a foreign Brad-
shaw, so the walking tour was abandoned, and
the friend rather congratulated himself on
escaping such a mournful companion.

When Autumn came round with its many
temptations to Scotland, where the muir-fowl
were crowing about their heathery knolls, and
the red-deer sunning their fat backs on the
leeward side of the corrie, he did indeed avail
himself of certain invitations to the hospitable

North ; and the General, who could level rifle
or fowling-piece, breast a hill, or plunge
through a moss with his juniors by twenty
years, strove hard in fatigue of body to earn
repose for the mind. But he did not stay long ;
the grand, grave beauty of those silent hills
oppressed and tortured him. He pitied the
wild old cock, flapping its life out on its own
purple heather, fifty yards off, mowed down by
his deadly barrel, even as it rose. When he
had stalked the "muckle red hart," with
antlered front of royalty, and three inches of
fat on those portly sides, up the burn, and
under the waterfall, and through the huge grey
boulders of eternal rock, to sight the noble
beast fairly, from a windward ambush, and
bring it down, pierced through the heart with
a long and "kittle" shot, his triumph was all
merged in sorrow for the dead monarch lying

so calm and stately in the quiet glen, not perhaps without a something of envy, for a creature thus insensible, and at rest for evermore.

The foresters wondered to see him in no way triumphant, and when they heard next morning he was gone, shook their heads, opining that "It was a peety! She was a pratty shot, and a fery tight shentlemans on a hill."

It was *work* the General required, not amusement; so he journeyed sadly back, to await in London the command he hoped would ere long recall him to a profession he had always loved, that seemed now to offer the sympathy and solace of a home.

Sometimes, but this only in moments of which he was ashamed, he would speculate on the possibility of meeting Miss Douglas by accident in the great city, and it soothed him

to fancy the explanations that would ensue.
He never dreamed of their resuming their old
footing; for the General's forbearance hitherto
had sprung from the strength, not the weakness
of his character, and the same stubborn gal-
lantry that held his position was available to
cover his defeat; but it would be a keen pleasure, he thought, though a sad one, to look in
her face just once more. After that he might
turn contentedly Eastward, go back into har-
ness, and never come to England again.

In the meantime, the days that dragged so
wearily with St. Josephs, danced like waves in
the sunshine through many of those other lives
with which he had been associated in his late
history. Amongst all gregarious animals, it
is the custom for a sick or wounded beast to
withdraw from the herd, who in no way concern
themselves about its fate, but continue their

browsings, baskings, croppings, waterings, and friskings, with a well-bred resignation to another's plight worthy of the human race. If the General's friends and acquaintance asked each other what had become of him, and waited for an answer, they were satisfied with the conventional surmise—

" Gone to Scotland, I fancy. They tell me it's a wonderful year for grouse ! "

Mrs. Lushington, yachting at Cowes, and remaining a good deal at anchor, because it was " blowing fresh outside," thought of him perhaps more than anybody else. Not that she felt the least remorseful for the break-up she believed to have originated solely in her own manœuvres. She was persuaded that her information conveyed through the anonymous letter had aroused suspicions which, becoming certainties on inquiry, detached him from

Satanella, and, completely mistaking his character, considered it impossible but that their
dissolution of partnership originated with the
gentleman. How the lady fared interested her
but little, and in conversation with other dearest
friends, she usually summed up the fate of this
one by explaining—

" It was *impossible* to keep poor Blanche
straight. Always excitable, and unlike other
people, you know. Latterly, I am afraid, *more*
than flighty, my dear, and *more* than odd."

Besides, Mrs. Lushington, as usual, had a
great deal of business on hand. For herself
and her set Cowes was nothing in the world
but London gone down to the sea. Shorter
petticoats, and hats instead of bonnets, made
the whole difference. There were the same
attractions, the same interests, the same in-
trigues. Even the same bores went to and

fro, and bored, as they breathed, more ·freely
in the soft, Channel air. Altogether, it was
fresher and quieter, but, if possible, stupider
than Pall Mall.

Nevertheless, Mrs. Lushington being in her
natural element, exercised her natural functions.
She was hard at work, trying to mate Bessie
Gordon, nothing loth, with a crafty widower,
who seemed as shy of the bait as an old
gudgeon under Kew Bridge. She had under-
taken, in conspiracy with other frisky matrons,
to spoil poor Rosie Barton's game with young
Wideacres, the catch of the season; and they
liked each other so well that this job alone
kept her in constant employment. She had
picnics to organise, yachting-parties to arrange,
and Frank to keep in good-humour; the latter
no easy task, for Cowes bored him extremely,
and, to use his own words, "he wished the

whole place at the devil!" She felt also vexed and disappointed that the General had withdrawn himself so entirely from the sphere of her attractions, reflecting that she saw a great deal more of him before he was free. Added to her other troubles, was the unpardonable defection of Soldier Bill. That volatile Light Dragoon had never been near her since Daisy's marriage—a ceremony in which he took the most lively interest, comporting himself as "best man" with an unparalleled audacity, and a joyous flow of spirits, that possessed, for a gathering composed of lively Hibernians, the greatest attractions. People said, indeed, that Bill had shown himself not entirely unaffected by the charms of a lovely bridesmaid, the eldest of Lady Mary's daughters; and it was impossible to over-estimate the danger of his position under such suggestive circumstances as must arise from a wedding in the house.

Then a grey hair or two had lately shown themselves in her abundant brown locks; while of the people she chose to flirt with, some neglected her society for a cruise, others afforded her more of the excitement produced by rivalry than she relished. None paid her the devoted attention she had learned to consider her due. Altogether, Mrs. Lushington began to find life less *couleur de rose* than she could wish, and to suspect the career she had adopted was not conducive to happiness, or even comfort. Many people make the same discovery when it is too late to abandon the groove in which they have elected to run.

Daisy, in the meantime, true to his expressed intention of turning over a new leaf, found no reason to be dissatisfied with his

lot. You might search Ireland through, and
it is saying a good deal, without finding a
more joyous couple than Captain and Mrs.
Walters. The looked-for promotion arrived at
last, and the bridegroom had the satisfaction
of seeing himself gazetted to a troop on the
very morning that provided him with a wife.
Old Macormac was pleased, Lady Mary was
pleased, everybody was pleased. The Castle
blazed with light and revelry, the tenants
drank, danced, and shouted. The " boys "
burnt the mountain with a score of bonfires,
consuming whiskey, and breaking each other's
heads to their own unbounded satisfaction. In
short, to use the words of Peter Corrigan, the
oldest solvent tenant on the estate, "The
masther's wedding was a fool to't! May I
never see glory av' it wasn't betther divarsion
than a wake!"

But Norah's gentle heart, even in her own new-found happiness, had a thought for the beautiful and stately Englishwoman, whom, if she somewhat feared her as a rival, she yet loved dearly as a friend.

"What's gone with her, Daisy?" she asked her young husband, before they had been married a fortnight. "Sure she would never take up with the nice old gentleman, a general he was, that marked the race-cards for us at Punchestown. Oh, Daisy! how I cried that night, because you didn't win!"

They were walking by the river-side, where they landed the big fish at an early period of their acquaintance, and Norah brought the gaff to bear in more ways than she suspected; where they parted so hopelessly, when, because of his very desolation, the true and generous girl had consented to plight him her troth;

and where they had hardly dared to hope they would meet again in such a glow of happiness as shone round them to-day. It was bright spring weather when they wished each other that sorrowful good-bye. Now, the dead leaves were falling thick and fast in the grey autumn gloom. Nevertheless, this was the real vernal season of joy and promise for both those loving hearts.

"What a goose you were to back me!" observed Daisy, with a pressure of the arm that clung so tight round his own. "It served you right, and, I hope, cured you of betting once for all!"

"That's no answer to my question," persisted Mrs. Walters. "I'm asking you to tell me about my beautiful Blanche Douglas, and why wouldn't the old General marry her if she'd have him."

"That's it, dear," replied her husband; "she

wouldn't have him! She—she accepted him, I *know*, and then she threw him over."

"What a shame!" exclaimed Norah. "Though, to be sure, he might have been her father." Then a shadow passed over her fair young brow, and she added wistfully, "Ah, Daisy! I'm thinking I know who she wanted all the time."

"Meaning *me?*" said Daisy, with a frank, saucy smile, that brought the mirth back to her face, and the sunshine to her heart.

"Meaning *you*, sir!" she repeated playfully. "But it's very conceited of you to think it, and very wrong to let it out. It's not so wonderful, after all," she added, looking proudly in his handsome young face: "I suppose I'm not the only girl that's liked you, dear, by a many. I oughtn't to expect it!"

"The only one that's *landed* the fish!" laughed Daisy, stopping in the most effectual manner

a little sigh, with which she was about to conclude her peroration. " You're mistaken about
Miss Douglas, though," he added, " I give
you my word. She hadn't your good taste, my
dear, and didn't *see* it! Look, Norah, there's
the very place I left Sullivan's fishing-rod.
He'll never get it again, so it's lucky I bought
his little brown horse. I wonder who found it.
What a day that was! Norah, do you remember ?"

" *Remember!* "

So the conversation turned on that most
interesting of topics—themselves, and did not
revert to Satanella nor her doings. If Norah
was satisfied, Daisy felt no wish to pursue
the subject. However indiscreet concerning his
successes, I think when a man has been refused by another lady, he says nothing about it
to his wife.

CHAPTER XXIX.

UNDIVIDED.

THE late autumn was merging into early winter, that pleasantest of all seasons for those sportsmen who exult in the stride of a good horse, and the stirring music of the hound. Even in Pall Mall true lovers of the chase felt stealing over them the annual epidemic, which winter after winter rages with unabated virulence, incurable by any known remedy. A sufferer—it would be a misnomer to call him a *patient*—from this November malady was gaping at a print-shop window, near the bottom of St. James's Street, wholly engrossed in the performances of a very bright bay horse, with a high-coloured rider, flying an impossible fence, surrounded by happy hunting-grounds, where perspective seemed unknown.

"D'ye think he'll get over, Bill?" said a familiar voice, that could only belong to Daisy Walters, who had stolen unperceived behind his friend.

"Not if the fool on his back can pull him into it," answered the other indignantly. And these comrades, linking arms, turned eastward, in the direction of their Club.

"How's the Missis?" said Bill, whose boast it was that he never forgot his manners.

"Fit as a fiddle," replied the happy husband. "Had a long letter from Molly this morning. Sent her best love—no, scratched that out, and desired to be kindly remembered to *you*."

Molly, called after Lady Mary, was the eldest, and, in Bill's opinion, the handsomest daughter, so he changed the subject with rather a red face.

"About to-morrow, now," said Bill. "I've got Martingale to do my orderly. Are you game for a day with the stag?"

"Will a duck swim!" was the answer. "Norah is coming too. I shall mount her on Boneen. He's own brother to the little horse that beat us at Punchestown."

"Couldn't do better in that country," asserted his friend. "He'll carry her like a bird, if she'll wake him up a bit, and it's simply *impossible* to get him down. By Jove, Daisy, there's St. Josephs going into the Club. How seedy he looks, and how old! Hang me, if I won't offer him a mount to-morrow. I wonder if he'll come?"

So this kind-hearted young sportsman, in

whose opinion a day's hunting was the panacea
for all ills, mental or bodily, followed his senior
into the morning-room, and proffered his best
horse, with the winning frankness of manner
that his friends found it impossible to resist.

"He's good enough to carry the Commander-
in-Chief," said Bill. " I've more than I can ride
till I get my long leave. I should be *so* proud if
you'd have a day on him ; and if he makes a mistake, I'll give him to you. There!"

St. Josephs was now on the eve of departure for the employment he had solicited.
While his outfit was preparing, the time hung
heavy on his hands, and he had done so many
kindnesses by this young subaltern that he felt
it would be only graceful and friendly to accept
a favour in return, so he assented willingly, and
Bill's face glowed with pleasure.

"Don't be late," said he. "Nine o'clock train

from Euston. Mind you get into the drop-carriage, or they'll take you on to the Shires. I'll join you at Willesden. And if we don't have a real clinker, I'll make a vow never to go hunting again."

Then he departed on certain errands of his own connected with the pugilistic art, and the General reflected sadly how it was a quarter of a century since he used to feel as keen as that reckless, light-hearted boy.

He waited on high authorities at the War Office, dined with a field-marshal, and, through a restless night, dreamed of Satanella, for the first time since her disappearance.

A foggy November morning, and a lame horse in the cab that took him to Euston Station did not serve to raise his spirits. But for Bill's anticipations of "a clinker," and the disappointment he knew it would cause that enthusiast, the General might have turned back to spend one more day in vain brooding and regret. Arrived on the platform, however, he got into a large saloon-carriage, according to directions, and found himself at once in the midst of so cheerful a party that he felt it impossible to resist the fun and merriment of the hour.

St. Josephs was too well-known in general society not to find acquaintances even here, though he was hardly prepared to meet representatives of so many pursuits and professions, booted and spurred for the chase, and, judging by the ceaseless banter they interchanged,

"All determined to ride, each resolved to be first."

Soldiers, sailors, diplomatists, bankers, lawyers, artists, authors, men of pleasure, and men of business, holding daily papers they never looked at, were all talking across each other,

and laughing incessantly, while enthroned at
one end of the carriage sat the best sportsman
and most. popular member of the assemblage,
whose opinions, like his horses, carried great
weight, and were of as unflinching a nature as
his riding, so that he was esteemed a sort of
president in jack-boots. Opposite him was
placed pretty Irish Norah, now Mrs. Walters,
intensely excited by her first appearance at
what she called "an English hunt," while she
imparted to Daisy, in a mellower brogue than
usual, very original ideas on things in general,
and especially on the country through which
they were flying at the rate of forty miles an
hour.

"It's like a garden where it's in tillage, and
a croquet-lawn where it's in pasture," said
Norah, after a gracious recognition of the
General, and cordial greeting to Bill, who was

bundled in at Willesden, panting, with his spurs in his hand. "Ah! now, Daisy, it's little of the whip poor Boneen will be wanting for easy leaps like them."

"Wait till you get into the Vale," said Daisy; "and whatever you do, let his head alone. Follow me close, and if I'm down, ride over me: it's the custom of the country."

The General smiled.

"I haven't been there for twenty years," said he; "but I can remember in my time we were not very particular. I shall follow my old friend," he added, nodding to the president, whose nether garments were of the strongest and most workmanlike materials; "when a man has no regular hunting things, he wants a leader to turn the thorns, and from all I hear, if I can only stick to mine, I shall be in a very good place."

Everybody agreed to this, scanning the speaker with approving glances the while. St. Josephs, though wearing trousers and a common morning coat, had something in his appearance that denoted the practised horseman, and when he talked of "twenty years ago," his listeners gave him credit for those successes which, in all times, are attributed to the men of the past.

"Mrs. Walters must be a little careful at the doubles," hazarded a quiet good-looking man who had not yet spoken, but whose nature it was to be exceedingly courteous where ladies were concerned. "A wise horse that knows its own rider is everything in the Vale."

Norah looked in the speaker's dark eyes with a quaint smile.

"Ah, then! if the horse wasn't wiser than the rider," said she, "it's not many leaps any of us would take without a fall!" and in the general laughter provoked by this incontestable assertion, a slight jerk announced that their carriage was detached from the train, and they had arrived.

Though it requires a long time to settle a lady in the saddle for hunting, even when in the regular swing of twice or thrice a week, and though Norah was about to enjoy her first gallop of the season, in a new habit, on a new horse, 'she and Daisy had ample leisure for a sober ride to the place of meeting, arriving cool and calm, pleased with the weather, the scenery, the company, and, above all, delighted with Boneen.

They were accompanied by the General on a first-class hunter belonging to Bill, and soon overtaken by its owner, who, having lingered behind to jump a four-year-old over a tempting stile for educational purposes, had crushed a new hat, besides daubing his coat, in the process.

"Down already!" said St. Josephs. "What happened to him? What did he do?"

"Rapped very hard," answered Bill; "found his friend at home, and went in without waiting to be announced;" but he patted the young pupil on its neck, and promised to teach it the trade before Christmas, nevertheless. Certainly, if practice makes perfect, no man should have possessed a stud of cleverer fencers than Soldier Bill.

And now, as she reached the summit of a grassy ascent, there broke on Norah's vision so extensive and beautiful a landscape as elicited an exclamation of amazement and delight.

Mile after mile, to the grey horizon, stretched a sweep of smooth wide pastures, intersected by massive hedges, not yet bare of their summer luxuriance, dotted by lofty standard trees, rich in the gaudy hues of autumn, lit up by flashes of a winding stream, that gleamed here and there under the willows with which its banks were fringed. Enclosures varying from fifty to a hundred acres gave promise of as much galloping as the heart of man, or even woman, could desire. And scanning those fences, the Irish lady admitted to herself, though not to her companions, that from a distance they looked as formidable obstacles as any she had confronted in Kildare.

"It's beautiful!" said Norah. "It's made on purpose for a hunt. Look, Daisy, there are the hounds! Oh, the darlings! And little Boneen, he sees them, too!"

Gathered round their huntsman, a wiry sporting-looking man on a thorough-bred bay horse, they were moving into sight from behind a hay-stack that stood in a corner of the neighbouring field. Rich in colour, beautiful in shape, and with a family likeness pervading the lot as if they were all one litter, a fox-hunter would have grudged them for the game they were about to pursue—a noble red-deer, in so far tame, that he was fed in a paddock, and brought to a condition that could tax the speed and endurance even of this famous pack. The animal had already arrived in a large van on wheels, drawn by a pair of horses, and surrounded by a levee of gaping rustics, whose eagerness and love for the sport reminded Norah of her countrymen on the other side of the Channel.

"Will they let him out here, Daisy?" said she, in accents of trembling excitement. "I wish they'd begin. What are we waiting for?"

"Your patience will not be tried much longer," said the General, lighting a cigar.

" Here comes the Master, at a pace that looks as if the mare that landed him the Thousand Guineas, the Oaks, and the St. Leger, had been made a cover-hack for the occasion ! "

" With the Derby-winner of the same year for second horse ! " added her husband. " If you want a pilot, Norah, you couldn't do better than stick to *him*, heavy as he is ! "

" I mean to follow *you*, sir," was the rejoinder. " If you don't mind, Daisy, may-be I'll be before ye."

Even while she spoke a stir throughout the whole cavalcade, and a smothered shout from the foot-people, announced that the deer had been enlarged.

With a wild leap in the air, as though rejoicing in recovered liberty, the animal started off at speed, but in the least favourable direction it could have taken, heading towards the ascent on the side of which the horsemen and a few carriages were drawn up. Then slackened its pace to a jerking, springing trot — paused — changed its mind — lowered its head — dashed wildly down the hill to disappear through a high thick bull-finch, and after a few seconds came again into view, travelling swift and straight across the Vale.

The General smoked quietly, but his eye brightened, and he seemed ten years younger for the sight.

"It's all right now," said he; "the sooner they lay them on the better."

Soldier Bill, drawing his girths, looked up with a beaming smile.

"They say there's a lady, a mysterious unknown, in a thick veil, who beats everybody with these hounds," he observed. "I wonder why she's not out to-day."

" I think she *is,*" replied Daisy, shooting a
mischievous glance at his wife. "1 fancied I
caught the flutter of a habit just now behind the
hay-stack. I suppose she's determined to get
a good start and cut Norah down ! "

Ere the latter could reply, the hounds dashed
across the line of the deer. Throwing their
tongues in full musical notes, they spread like a
fan, with noses in the air ; then, stooping to the
scent, converged, in one melodious crash and
chorus, ere they took to running with a grim,
silent determination that denoted the extremity
of pace. Every man set his horse going at
speed. Nearly a dozen selected their places in
the first fence—a formidable bull-finch. The
rest, turning rather away from the hounds,
thundered wildly down to an open gate.

Amongst those who meant riding straight,
it is needless to say, were Mrs. Walters and

her three cavaliers. These landed in the second field almost together. Daisy, closely pursued by his wife, stealing through a weak place under a tree. The General sailing fairly over all, and Bill, unable to resist the temptation of a gap, made up with four strong rails, getting to the right side with a scramble that wanted very little of a nasty fall.

The hounds were already a quarter of a mile ahead, with nobody near them but a lady on a black hunter, who was well alongside, going, to all appearance, perfectly at her ease; while her groom, on a chesnut horse, left hopelessly behind, rode in the wake of the General, and wished he was at home.

Daisy, whose steeple-chasing experience had taught him never to lose his head, was the only one of our party who did not feel a little bewildered by the pace. Taking in everything at a glance, he observed the black hunter in front sail easily over a fence that few horses would have looked at. There was no mistaking the style and form of the animal. " Of course it is!" he muttered. " Satanella, by all that's inexplicable! We shall not catch them at *this* pace, however!" Then, pulling his horse to let his wife come up, he shouted in her ear, "Norah, that's Miss Douglas!"

Whether she heard him or not, the only answer Mrs. Walters vouchsafed was to lean back in her saddle and give Boneen a refresher with the whip.

Unlike a fox, whose reasons are logical and well considered, a deer will sometimes turn at right angles for no conceivable cause, pursuing the new line with as much speed and decision as the old.

In the present instance the animal, after

leaping a high thorn fence with two ditches, broke short off in a lateral direction, under the very shadow of the hedge it had just cleared, and at the pace they were going the hounds, as a natural consequence, over-ran the scent.

Miss Douglas pulled up her horse, and did not interfere. There being, fortunately, no one to assist them, they flung themselves beauti- fully, swinging back to the line and taking it up again with scarcely the loss of a minute. The President, two fields off, struggling hard to get nearer, was perhaps the only man out who sufficiently appreciated their steadiness. Like Coleridge's Ancient Mariner, "he blessed them unaware." Bill, I fear, did the *other* thing, for the fence was so high he never saw them turn, and jumped well into their midst, happily without doing any damage.

This slight delay, however, had the effect of

bringing Daisy, his wife, Soldier Bill, and the
General into the same field with Miss Douglas.
She heard the footfall of their horses, looked
round, and set the black mare going faster than
before. If—as, indeed, seemed probable—she
was resolved not to be overtaken, the pack,
streaming away at speed once more, served her
purpose admirably. No horse alive could catch
them; and Satanella herself seemed doing her
best to keep on tolerable terms at that terrific
pace. The majority of the field had already
been hopelessly distanced. The General found
the superior animal he rode fail somewhat
in the deep holding meadows. Bill was in
difficulties, although he had religiously adhered
to the shortest way. Even Daisy began to
wish for a pull, and only little Boneen, quite
thorough-bred, and as good as he was sluggish,
kept galloping on, strong and full of running

as at the start. For more than a mile our friends proceeded with but a slight alteration in their relative positions—Satanella, perhaps, gradually leaving her followers, and the hounds drawing away from all five. In this order two or three flying fences were negotiated, and a fair brook cleared. Daisy, looking back in some anxiety, could not but admire the form in which Norah roused and handled Boneen. That good little horse, bred and trained in Ireland, seemed to combine the activity of a cat with the sagacious instincts of a dog. Like all of his blood, he only left off being lazy when his companions began to feel tired; and Mrs. Walters, coming up with her husband, as they rose the hill from the waterside, declared, though he did not hear her, " I could lead the hunt now, Daisy, if you'd let me. Little Boneen's as pleased as Punch! He'd like to

pull hard, only he's such a good boy he doesn't
know how!"

Bill's horse dropped its hind legs in the
brook, and fell, but was soon up again with
its rider. The General got over successfully;
nevertheless, his weight was beginning to tell,
and the ground being now on the ascent, he
found himself the last of the five people with
the hounds.

At the crest of the hill frowned a black,
forbidding-looking bull-finch: on this side a
strong rail; on the other, if a horse ever got
there, *the uncertainty*, which might or might
not culminate in a rattling fall. Daisy glanced
anxiously to right and left, on his wife's behalf,
but there was no forgiveness. They must have
it, or go home! Then he watched how the
famous black mare would acquit herself a
hundred yards ahead of him, and felt little

reassured to detect such a struggle in the air while she topped the fence, as by no means inferred a pleasant landing where she disappeared on its far side.

He wavered, he hesitated, and pulled his horse off for a stride; but Norah's impatient "Ah, Daisy! go on now!" urged him to the attempt, and he *chanced* it, with his heart in his mouth, for her sake, not his own.

Taking fast hold of his horse's head, he got over with a scramble, turning afterwards in the saddle to watch how it fared with his wife and little Boneen. Her subsequent account described the performance better than could any words of mine.

"When I loosed him off at it," said she, "I just touched him on the shoulder with the whip, to let him know he wasn't in Kildare. He understood well enough, the little darling!

for he pricked his ears, and came back to a slow canter; but I'd like ye to have felt the bound he made when he rose to it! Such a place beyond! 'Twas as thick as a cabbage-garden—dog-roses, honeysuckles, I'm not sure there wasn't cauliflowers, and all, twisted up together to conceal a deep, wide, black-looking hole, like a borcen.* Well, I just felt him give a sort of a kick, while he left the entire perplexity ten feet behind him, and when he landed, as light as a fairy, Daisy, I'm sure I heard him laugh!"

Mrs. Walters, like most of her nation, abounded in enthusiasm. She could not forbear a little cry of delight at the panorama that opened before her, when she had effected the above-mentioned feat. To the very horizon

---

* "Borcen,"—Irish for a deep, stone-paved lane.

lay stretched a magnificent vale of pasture, brightened by the slanting rays of a November sun. Far ahead, fleeting across the level below, sped a dark object, she recognised for the deer; a field nearer were the hounds, running their hardest, in a string that showed they too had caught sight of their game. Half-way down the hill she was herself descending the other lady was urging the black mare to headlong speed, very dangerous on such a steep incline. Fifty yards behind Satanella came Daisy, and close on his heels, Norah, wild with delight, feeling a strong inclination to give Boneen his head, and go by them all. The little horse, however, watched his stable-companion narrowly, while his rider's eyes were riveted on the hounds. Suddenly she felt him shorten his stride and stop, with a jerk, that nearly shot her out of the saddle. Glancing at Daisy, for an explanation, she screamed aloud, and covered her face with her hands.

When she looked again, she was aware of her husband's horse staring wildly about with the bridle over its head; of Daisy himself on foot; and a few yards off the good black mare prostrate, motionless, rolled up in a confused and hideous mass with her hapless rider.

Down hill, at racing pace, Satanella had put her fore-feet through a covered drain, with the inevitable result—the surface gave way, letting her in to the shoulders, and a few yards farther on, she lay across her mistress, with her neck broken, never to stir those strong, fleet limbs again.

"Oh! Daisy, they're both killed!" whispered Norah, with a drawn, white face, while her husband, busying himself to undo the girths, and thus extricate that limp, helpless figure from beneath the weight that crushed it so sorely, shouted for assistance to Soldier Bill and the General, who at that moment entered the field together.

"I trust in heaven *not!*" he replied aloud; and, below his breath, even while his heart smote him for the thought, "It might have been worse. My darling, it might have been *you!*"

CHAPTER XXX.

THE BITTER END.

IT was indeed a sad sight for those joyous riders, exulting but a moment before in all the triumph and excitement of their gallop. Saddest and most pitiable for the General, thus to find and recognise the woman he had loved and lost. While they took her gently out from under the dead mare's carcase, she groaned feebly, and they said, "Thank God!" for at least there seemed left a faint spark of life. Assistance, too, was near at hand. As Norah observed, "'Twasn't like Kildare, where ye wouldn't have seen a shealing or may be so much as a potato-garden for miles. But every farm here was kept like a domain, and they'd built a dwelling-house almost in every field." Within a short distance stood the comfortable mansion, surrounded by its well-stocked fold-yards, of a substantial yeoman; and Bill, with two falls, was there in two minutes! A few of the second flight also, persevering resolutely on the line the hounds had gone, straggled up and did good service. What became of the Field, and where the deer was taken, none of these had opportunity to ascertain. All their energies, all their sympathies, were engrossed by that helpless, motionless form, that beautiful rigid face, so wan and white, beneath its folds of glossy raven hair.

Carrying her softly and carefully on a gate to her place of shelter, it looked as if they formed a funeral procession, of which the General seemed chief-mourner.

His bearing was stern and composed, his step never faltered, nor did his hand shake; but he who wrestled with the angel of old, and prevailed against him, could scarcely have outdone this loving, longing heart in earnestness of purpose and passionate pleading of prayer.

"But once more!" was his petition. "Only that she may know me, and look on me once more!" And it was granted.

For two days Blanche Douglas neither spoke nor stirred. Mrs. Walters constituted herself head nurse, and never left her pillow. The General remained the whole time at the threshold of her chamber.

The surgeon, a country practitioner of high repute, who saw her within an hour of her accident, committed himself to no opinion by

word or sign, but shook his head despondingly
the moment he found himself alone. The
famous London doctor, telegraphed for at once,
preserved an ominous silence. He, too, getting
into the fly that took him back to the station,
looked grave and shook his head. The hospitable yeoman, who placed his house and all
he had freely at the sufferer's disposal, packing
off the very children to their aunt's, at the
next farm, felt, as he described it, "Down-
hearted—uncommon." His kindly wife went
about softly and in tears. Daisy and Bill
hurried to and fro, in every direction, as required, by night and day; while Norah, watching in the darkened room, tried to hope
against hope, and pray for that which she
dared not even think it possible could be
granted.

The General looked the quietest and most

composed of all. Calm and still, he seemed less to watch than to wait. Perhaps some subtler instinct than theirs taught him the disastrous certainty, revealed to him the inevitable truth.

Towards evening of the second day Norah came into the passage and laid her hand on his shoulder, as he sat gazing vacantly from the window, over the fields and orchards about the farm. They loomed hazy and indistinct in the early winter twilight, but the scene on which he looked was clear enough—a bright sunny slope, a golden gleam in the sky above, and on earth a dark heap, with a trailing habit, and a slender riding-whip clenched in a small gloved hand.

"She has just asked for you," whispered Norah. "Go to her—quick! God bless you, General! Try and bear it like a man!"

The room was very dark. He stole softly to her bedside, and felt his fingers clasped in the familiar clinging touch once more.

" My darling!" he murmured, and the strong man's tears welled up, thick and hot, like a child's.

Her voice came, very weak and low. " The poor mare!" she said; "is she much hurt? It was no fault of hers."

He must have answered, and told her the truth without knowing it; for she proceeded, more feebly than before.

" Both of us! Then it's no use. I was going to give her to you, dear, and ask you to take care of her for my sake. Have you—have you forgiven?"

" Forgiven!" His failing accents were even less steady than her own.

" I vexed you dreadfully," she continued.

"I was not good enough for you. I see it all; and, if it could come again, I would never leave you—never! But I did it for the best. I took great pains to hide myself away down here; but I'm glad—yes, I'm very glad you found me out at last. How dark it is! Don't let go my hand. Kiss me, my own! I know now that I *did* love you dearly—far better than I thought."

The feeble grasp tightened, stronger, stronger yet. The shadows fell, the night came down, and a pale moon threw its ghostly light into the chamber. But the face he loved was fixed and grey now, the hand he clasped was stiff and cold in death!

The General carried to India a less sore heart, perhaps, than he had expected. There was no room left for the gnawing anxiety, the bitter sense of humiliation, the persistent struggle against self, that distressed and troubled him in his previous relations with her he had loved so dearly, and lost so cruelly even in the hour she became his own. He was grave and silent, no doubt; in feelings and appearance, many years beyond his real age; but every fresh grey hair, every additional symptom of decay, seemed only a mile-stone nearer home. Without speculating much on its locality, he cherished an ardent hope that soon he might follow to the place where she had gone before. None should come between them there, he thought, and they need never part again.

Soldier Bill and Daisy saw the last of him when he left England: the former rather envied every one who was bound for a sphere in which there seemed a possibility of seeing real service; the latter comparing his senior's lonely life and blighted hopes with his own happy lot, felt a humbler, a wiser, and a better man for the contrast.

Mrs. Walters, though losing none of her good-nature and genial Irish humour, became more staid in manner, altogether more matronly; and though she went out hunting on occasion, certainly rode less boldly than before the catastrophe. Her sister Mary, however, who came over to stay with her about this time, kept up the family credit for daring, and would have taken Bill's heart by storm (if she had not won it already) with the fearlessness she displayed in following him over the most formidable obstacles. After a famous day on Boncen, when she bustled that lazy little gentleman along in a manner that perfectly electrified him, Bill could hold out no longer, but placed himself, his fortunes, Catamount, and

Benjamin, at her disposal. All these she was good enough to accept but the badger; and that odorous animal was compelled to evacuate his quarters in the wardrobe for a more suitable residence out of barracks, at a livery-stable. So they were married in London, and inaugurated the first day of their honeymoon by a quick thing with the Windsor drag-hounds.

Of Mrs. Lushington there is little more to be said. The sad fate of her former friend she accepted with the resignation usually displayed by those of her particular set, in the face of such afflictions as do not immediately affect themselves and their pleasures. She vowed it was very sad, talked of wearing black—but didn't! and went out to dinner much as usual. Even Bessie Gordon showed more feeling, for she *did* cry when she heard the news, and appeared that night at a ball with swollen eyelids and a red place under her nose. Many people asked what had become of Miss Douglas? The answer was usually something to this effect—

"Don't you remember? Painful business; shocking accident. Killed out hunting. Odd story; odd girl. Yes—handsome, but very peculiar style."

They buried the good black mare where she fell. Long before the grass was green over her grave rider and horse had been very generally forgotten. Yet in their own circle both had created no small sensation in their time. But life is so far like the chase, that it admits of but little leisure for hesitation; none whatever for regret. How should we ever get to the finish if we must needs stop to pick up the fallen, or to mourn for the dead?

In certain kind and faithful hearts, however,

it is but justice to say the memory of that hapless pair remains fresh and vivid as on the day of their fatal downfall.

There is a stern, grey-headed soldier in the East who sees Blanche Douglas nightly in his dreams; and Daisy Walters, in his highest state of exultation, when he has been well-carried, as often happens, through a run, heaves a sigh, and feels something aching at his heart, that recalls the black mare and her lovely wayward rider, while it reminds him in a ghostly whisper that "there never was one yet like Satanella!"

THE END.

VIRTUE AND CO., PRINTERS, CITY ROAD, LONDON.

www.ingramcontent.com/pod-product-compliance
Lightning Source LLC
Chambersburg PA
CBHW030634030726
47497CB00006B/1776